FOOD FOR THE DEAD.
BECAUSE THE LIVING...
DON'T NEED IT!

A collection of Poems and Micro stories by

L.F. Young

ISBN-13: 9781234567890
ISBN-10: 1477123456

Cover design by: Art Painter
Library of Congress Control Number: 2018675309
Printed in the United States of America

NOTE FROM THE AUTHOR

Thank you very much for purchasing this book of poems and micro stories. These are a collection of some of my poems and micro stories I've done over the years. I hope you find them enjoyable and maybe even helpful, if you too are going through hard times. As i have and as I still do, in this thing we call life.

So, what is a micro story you might ask. Well its a smaller version of a short story, but it doesn't have the required word limit to be called a short story. So, in my infinite wisdom (LOL) I came up with my own term. Micro story... I don't know about you, but I think it just might ketch on.

Why did I put poems and micro stories together you might ask. Well, it just seemed the right thing to do. So, happy reading and thank you agian for purchasing my book.

PROLOGUE

"Give us a bite, my master."

"No. It's not ready, and I'm not your master. I'm a humble purveyour, of words and creative stories."

"Please, my master. We thirst for more of your words."

"Well... maybe a nibble. You creatons of the lost."

"Oh thank you, thank you my master. We of the dead, don't deserve your devin words of faith and hope. But as we read your cherished gifts, we pray to be of the living... one day. Someday!"

"In time, in time my children. You, with the forgotten and drained souls. You, who wonder the wastelands of lost dreams. Read my work and feel alive again. Walk out of the stygian world you've tumbled into and rise to the light of hope and faith. Not in me, but in your fellow mankind and firstly in yourself. Rise you dead wondering souls and take back your lives."

****

What is true happiness?
16 March 2020

Question:

Live life one second at a time, for when it's gone you'll never get it back. Immortality lies in a pure second of true happiness. But what is, living in the moment... living this very second, even mean?

It means:

To make a wish, hold it for a lifetime. Then throw it away, praying it will start over again the very next day. And in that wish, you ponder a million chances... to do it all again. But, only right the next day.

A second, is a blessing. Given to all of the children of this Earth. In the hopes, that we will wish to do it all again. But in the right way and the right time. Without greed, anger and envy. Controlling the minds and hearts of humanity.

For you see. The light of humanity is that wish, becoming that second. If only we try.

****

"Did you like your treat, my children of the lost? Are you ready for more?"

"Oh yes, my master."

"Then have at it, gorge yourselves on my profound writings. Now feast, upon the full corse meal... my lovelies. And I'm not your master for crying out loud."

FOOD FOR THE DEAD, BECAUSE THE LIVING… DON'T NEED IT!

Book One
A collection of poems and micro stories by

L.F. Young

CONTENTS

1.

Truest of kisses
28 April 2012

Flows far wider
then the vast openness
of the endless sea
lays far smoother
then the richest fabric
of the rarest silk worm.

Burns far hotter

then the ever glowing heat
of the inextinguishable sun
caresses far sensual
then the sweetest rose
of the lushest vineyard.

Sings far louder
then the golden trumpet
of the great Dizzy Gillespie
truer by far
then anything of man
has ever created.

If only for the heavenly touch
of her ever graceful lips
my soul would be set free
if only for the one second, I...
were that ray of pure light
that gives rise to silken lips.

If only for the briefest of moments, I...
were the need for her hearts desire
in the simplest of caresses.
if only for the single beat of time, I...
were the chosen of all men
in knowing that pleasure of her embrace.

If only
if only
if only for one
sweet and sensual, everlasting kiss.

2.

I've grown so tired...
09 May 2010

Tired
I've expired my resolve, in these last three weeks.
Tired
in my worried soul, for emptiness is my only friend.

Age
has claimed, held and calls home to my youth.
Age
sets my feet in concrete, of despair and loss.

Release
calls from the sharpened blade,
small pill or bullets quick kill.
Release
solidifies my past to my future, with no hope for my now.

God
how your pitiful son has fallen, has tried and failed.
God
your son now hold loss-shame-sadness
in wrinkled hands of pain.

3.

The Pianist
25 March 2010

Motion, creates movement
the ever flowing hands, of a pianist
sending waves of pleasure, joy, emotion
to my soul, to my heart.

Where it relishes in the feel, and feeling
of the sound, and the passion
in the notes of pain, happiness, loss and love
through, the fingers of a maestro.

My soul swims in the melody
of its highs, its lows
in the motion, that's created in the movement
the openness... of the pianists creation and soul.

4.

Snow
15 may 2006

With the ease of snow, falling from a winter sky
I look into your eyes and wonder why
why, for all these years
I've been the luckiest husband-man-human to ever exist.

To have been blessed, by those winter eyes
and the love that falls down, like so
many snowy winter nights.
I pray each and every day for snow
for the cold days and chilly stormy nights.

I've been blessed, in having blue gray eyes to look into
and the warmth, of a lover's blood
coursing through the most beautiful
arms, ever to hold me tight
while I look outside, time to time at snowy flight.

So blow, winds of winter, keep it cold
all I ask is for mother natures grumpy winter,
to let it snow
blow winter blow, bring it on
snow... snow... snow...

5.

Autumn
04 October 2019

Falling rain of mother natures, faithful love
trees circling, around the heart of hope.
For leaves know, through the twists and turns of time
a leaf changes its path, its chime.

Falling leaves of rain, wash away my emptiness
set me free to float.
On coolness and everlasting hope
that's true, love will stay afloat.

Colors so strange, to the heart of darkness
earthiness to fresh, to see a scent on the breeze.
Whence, to you come from
where, have you been.

Winters angry fool. Shall stomp down all to soon
I have not as yet seen and felt all the leaves.
Fall leaves. From the clouds of trees
to clean and release the pure essence... that is me.

Stay. Oh please stay the crispy hand of Jack Frost
for I still wish to turn over every leaf.
That has yet to fall
yet to fall upon... me.

6.

Knock. Knock. Knock!
02 Oct 2009

The wanting of something, someone… drives the insanity of my reality to new levels of darkness and despair. Creating a world of illusions, thats changed and challenged the existence of my hopes, my dreams. Making the steps I take forward, to a new future all the more exacerbating.

Ghosts of the past take flight, darkening my vision. Holding onto the spectacle… that has become my life, my incomplete world. Little footsteps run through my mind, with the echoes of the inner daemon of my past. The one I've run from, run too.

In the youngest days of my confused life, it was he, she or possible it. That kept me safe, that kept me bound and confused. Keeping the dreams alive and far away from my reach. In all the years I've ventured down the dangers path, it was my inner daemon who stood by my side, whispering… constantly whispering little things.

Until I meet her, the lady of my hope, my passion and my destiny. She showed me love, she showed me faith in the warmth of a kiss and the love of a wish, until…

THE WHISPERS ARE BACK!

The inner daemon is knocking at the door of my conscience, requesting and audience, seeking a new foot hold. Angered. At the time we've spent apart and the chance I've taken at being one... one with peace.

It took a single moment in the not so far past, of my once happy home. To shatter all that I've worked for, desired on... peace. When she said I've lied, I've cheated and now I've drained your account dry. That was the first knock on the door.

Now the last foothold of myself, my faith, my peace is gone. With the passing of my beloved boxer Max. Passing away far to soon and far to fast. That was the second knocking on the door. Now the little inner daemon of my unconscious mind, whispers a lullaby, of new fears, new pains and the darkness yet to come.

Tempting me with safety, warmth and the protection of all I've yet to be. If I only let loose, let slip and release my hold. My peace. Setting free the inner daemon, that was once and will be...

AGAIN ME!

I hear the third and final knock. With my little daemon inside saying. One look, one wish, one chance at total bliss floating freely, in the temptation of my inner daemon saying let me out, I'll love you with a simple little kiss.

7.

Reaching. Are U the one?
15 Jan 2011

I reach out... to you. Hoping your my one. The one.
That will take away the darkness,
the pain, the loneliness.

Of years, upon years of emptiness. Ringing
all I am, out to the world
to see, hear and know. That a man
can change, can grow a soul.

Are you my soul mate? Are you the coming
of my future-my past?
Bringing life everlasting. In your
smile, your hug, your kiss.

I've been hoping... wishing. For someone
like you, an equal in all things.
A simple soul to match my own. No...! A better
soul, then I've ever known.

To fill this empty whole. A hole... I've called my home.
To bring a family, to the singularity of my single mind.

8.

I Scream. I've Screamed!
19 March 2010

I've screamed out to the very core of the world. A world that's keeping me in its spherical movement, holding me in its gravity of constant pain.

Constant misery and the ever constant sadness... I've screamed, and continue to scream to the heavens, to the very pillars of Gods shinning thrown.

Can anything ever take away this pain? Searing my soul, my flesh, my home... Pain, ever in my sight, in my taste, my hold. On this very fabric, that I've called home.

A home that I've lost in my soul... I've screamed. I scream. Out to the very foundation, of Gods heavenly face.

Why can't you take this pain away from me? Why can't you rain on me, rain over me? Why can't you just come down and pray with me...?

I scream. I've screamed. Will I always scream? Why can't you come down, and release this from me?

From the pain that I see, in the mirror. The face, in front of me. Constantly showing me, the failures I've achieved and the shame...

I scream. I've screamed! Lord heaven above, when are you going to come down and free, not just me... but all that is you, all that is we?

9.

Tooth and Claw
06 April 2010

In the crisp of the cool night
death... treads on silken paw
quiet as the pale horse
swift as the reapers blade.

In that split second
you look left... right...
pray to the up
fear the down.

Cross your I's and dot your T's
for the lion of fate
the tooth of reality
and the claw of finality... is coming!

10.

Your immortal day's
02 Feb 2010

Traveling through perdition's flame
he will come calling
your actions have been weighed
as he sits, upon his pale horse.

Your very words, hold merit
giving salvation-damnation...
by these, and these alone
you will be judged.

For brimstone, or golden rays
are kept in his heart
stored, locked away
till your time comes.

Held in his holy hand
is the sickle of destiny
and in its wake of passing
a glimpse will be given.

You shall see the golden gate
but sin will not let you in.
You shall see the flame of pain, despair
but love, friendship will not let you in.

Hope or hate
you'll be held accountable.

Saved or condemned
you'll be held accountable.

Till the end... of your immortal day's.

11.

When love strikes
22 Jan 2010

Loves unprecedented, insatiable and unknowing
in its wants, its needs
loves passion flows like the thunderstorm
striking at random... ripping, stripping.

Taking the walls down
of loneliness, pain and hurt
with the electricity of the moment
the look of a connection.

It only takes a flash, a moment
a split second, a strike
to fall in its everlasting hole
a pit, that most will never know.

True and absolute... love.

But when it strikes, its like fire
it lights up the darkness in your eyes
grabs, takes hold and ignites
your passion, your soul.

Most fear to ride the lightning
of loves thunderstorm
they run and hide, from its strike
fearing more, the threat of rejection.

They'd rather be one

of the lost and never known
one of the should-a-have
but were to afraid to grab, when its known.

Instead, grab that lightning rod
stand in the eye of the thunderstorm
scream to the heavens
saying... strike me, make all right.

For I no-longer wish to be alone
empty in my heart, lonely in my soul
quiet in my life, vacant in my home
tired of being destined, to roam alone.

12.

The ignorance of youth
27 Sept 2019

Ignorance is a powerful tool, in the making of man. It sends him down pathways, yet seen and yet known. But ignorance can also grow heavy, on an aged mined. When the passing of time, shows you all you've done wrong and all you could of had.

In my haste of flight, from that hell of a house I grew from. I chose a life of solitude and the knowledge, that my bloodline would end with me. How mistaken I have been, how sad I am now.

It took nearly fifty years of life's, nurturing, to show me the errors of my miss guided youth. It isn't my bloodline, that's been destroyed, it's been my innocence of hope.

In my attempts at gaining the knowledge, that I will be the last of her bloodline and it will end with me. Unknowingly I've followed her, down the razors edge, of hate and misery.

I've given her, the only thing that was truly mine... my heart. And by doing so, I've allowed that creature I called mother, the victory. In the knowledge that she, triumphed over me, that by allowing her to command my present.

She controlled my future!

By letting this so called knowledge, that I could end her bloodline. That I could stop any future offspring, of that cursed bloodline to exist. That I could win.

But in reality, I should have sired, multiple offspring's and taught them the ways I've come to know. That of patience, love for all things and being and honorable human being.

If... I had done this, I would of won. Instead of looking down the lonely pathway I've created for myself. Seeing the inevitable destiny. I've constructed. One of sadness, shame and emptiness.

So, with a heavy soul. I give birth to my own sort of creation... in my writings. And hope for the day my children will run, play and know a better future then their father did.

13.

The Family. Confused?
01 March 2010

If in singularity
happiness can't be found
never will there be
solidarity of clarity
in the wholeness and holiness
of the family.

Never will the whole
be one
when the I, feels alone
among the team
whether it be
friend, co-worker... family.

In all things, everything matters
the happiness of singularity
must reign supreme
or the peace of the family
will be nothing.

Nothing
nothing
nothing
but a dream!

14.

My Split Apart
04 Dec 2009

Its said, when the spirit's ready
friends will come.
Its said, when the heart's ready
love will come.

I've had years, in the spirit
only loneliness… came.
I've had openness, in the heart
only emptiness… came.

Every year turns to an end
and still, I wait.
Every new season, has a start-end
and still, I nurture my faith and fate.

That one day, the musses will send
a reason, to the madness.
That one day, two will meet-bond
a reason, turns into happiness.

Sending my, Split Apart
joining, hearts and friends.
Sending and end, to my empty heart
joining, creating room to transcend.

Come, my Split Apart
bringing, an end to our coy.

Come, the Eve to my heart
bringing, completion in our joy.

15.

The little door down the hall
14 Feb 2009

For all those who fear the closet,
fears whats under the bed
or the creaking noise
that bounces around in our head...

The house was to be sold. And I had to venture inside, too see if there was anything I wanted to keep and anything I wanted to be sold, at the estate sale a few days from now. It's been years since I came back to the old family farm house of my childhood days. I stood there outside the front door, lingering on a few memories of happier times, but trying to forget all the memories of the bad times.

A chill ran down my spine as the front door. I looked down the dark hallway of my old home and the darker memories of my past. I took those first few tentative steps, as I walked down the hallway coming to an old closet door. A door from where dreams were filled with evil things and deeds done all those years ago. With fear and sweat I reach out for the old copper door handle, while a cringe of panic sets in, but with determination and a shaking hand I open the old hallway closet door.

It creeks and squeaks telling of things yet to come, with one eye then two I peak inside, looking for my dad, who was taken all those years ago. They say the Boogie Man doesn't exist, but for all those who fear the door, the bed, or that noise in our head. We know... we know!

I reach up and pull the dusty string, the light goes on and fear is pushed back behind the old sweaters, jackets, balls and bats. Stepping inside I remember the past, when my dad closed the door and told me to count back. Starting with five then four and when you you get to one I'll open the closet door. He would say, all the while laughing and rapping on the closet door, as I prayed and said "Go away!".

"I told you, the Boogie Man doesn't exist, its all untrue. He's not behind the door, not under your bed and not in your little pathetic head." I heard more laughter coming from the crack, sliding under the hallway closet door.

With each number the stutter gets worse, panic sets in and my feet start to spin. Objects fall, grabbing, reaching, panic is no longer in the hall. I scream, I fall, while my father yells... "I can't hear you, are you counting at all?" I count, push back the fear, count, taste my tears. In the vain hope that this is not real, just a dream of forgotten youth and painful tears and hurtful years.

The wind blows from down the hall, slamming the door shut. Bringing me back to the present, while memories fade back. I turn reaching for the string, and stumble on a ball. Feeling the hand as I fall. Panic, fear and all those childhood years come back in a flash, a flood... It was all true, and once again I taste the tears. He has come back. From my forgotten years and all those things my dad said, that the Boogie Man wasn't real. He was wrong, and it is all true.

The Boogie Man does exist and he has come for me, as he will come for you too. I grabbed the door handle just in time. Daring myself to look back as I opened the door, I see his scared and bloody face looking at mine, I see his hand grabbing for mine. As I backed out the hallway closet door, all the while hearing him whispering those same words vile words so long ago.

"No, little boy this is no dream, and yes the Boogie Man does exist. And I've been waiting a very long time, to feast upon you."

Then another long ago memory comes back from all those years ago. Back then when I screamed and ran out the hallway closet door. From that same bloody hand, all those years ago. I remembered shoving my dad into the hallway closet and slamming the door.

Yelling to him. "Count, count fast and when you get to one, who knows maybe I'll hear your screams... as I walk out the front door."

The End!

16.

Self becoming
04 may 2018

The very nature of distraction
is the very essence
of one's destruction, of self awareness.

The absolute effect of awareness
is the collaboration
of millions of tiny distractions.

Only in destroying our distractions
will we become self aware
of our own limitations, of self becoming.

17.

Three little words
08 Jan 2011

-Now-

Moments of pain, flash through my mind
with those words... DON'T TOUCH ME!!!

After years apart, days alone
the night physically-emotionally
ripped asunder.

-Then-

Deployed to god knows where
waiting for the day
the plane finally comes home
home to my runway.

Seeing you, for the first time...
sang to me
the vision of your shining light
knowing I'm home tonight.

But, unknown to use
distance still held sway
keeping the emotions of yesterday's
far... far away.

Till, I tried to stimulate emotional bliss
pleasure
in nothing more, then a loving kiss.

Screams were yelled
from those precious-beautiful lips
the only ones, I've ever known
have only known.

DON'T TOUCH ME...!

For I've found another
who will-has taken your place.
I no-longer want you, in this-my home.

-Now-

Even now, after year's have gone by-bye.
I hear those words, and wonder
will I ever... have the heart to say goodbye.

And find someone else
to hold... to know
giving all my love
for the entire world, to know-show.

18.

When will death catch up?
05 Feb 2011

Long, has my wheel
been on the cog of life
running, running… ever on the go.
When will it come to and end?

Internally I'm dead
externally I'm singularly alone
emotionally I'm dysfunction-ally cold
physically I'm…

My soul has cried out
to this un-feeling, un-caring world
hoping, longing, needing
one single soul to call… friend.

When will times, understanding
come to a permanent, an everlasting end?
When will the grand hand of the Reaper
bring peace, bring death, to this lonely soul?

Until that succulent sweet day, rains down
on its eternal bed.
I'll sow, with out reap… reach, without greed
and pray, for the pain, to cease its resend.

For all in this life, has soured to its end
and still... the hand of death
has yet to come
giving me, a farewell send.

19.

The four seasons of Love's express train
04 Nov 2009

Spring

Winters bite is fading away. For love's in the air... and alls right with the world. That first glimpse of her/him sends shivers, making all hearts to quiver. Passion takes control as the winds of spring, shower the young with hopes of forever being loved... in spring. Loves new, loves young even childish in every way. But love found in spring... is destined to fade away.

Summer

Warming rays of the growing sun, shine down on the love started anew. Giving each to the other, letting passion fly as the dove does to the golden rays of a sunny day. Hearts sing with forever on the wind. Promises rain down, with the warmth of happy clouds, of love and hope. That, all will stay green, gold, bold... anew. But love found in summer... is destined to fade to blue, for its untrue.

Fall

Waring leaves of the coming northern breeze, fall down on hearts breathing in the change... from loneliness to hope. From the chilly memories of days gone bye, to the warmth of a new lovers heart. With the spell of falls magical glow of red, brown, green and gold. Giving rise to the notion, that alls well in the fall. That the arms of the lover, will hold back the northern winds of change. But love found in the fall… is destined to age.

Winter

Waiting hearts grow cold and freeze, with out the love of someone new… yet wait. What's that on the horizon, strong yet soft arms and hands to take hold of, and in the eager of the aging year. You let love settle in… long before the mind takes control. But love found in winter… is destined to wither-fade.

The new year

Heed these words of a simple soul, let not the love of one season take hold. Give love a chance to grow and know, each and every season. For what it has and what it holds, and if you find love anew in each season, with that special someone… Then, grab the last day of the old year and say goodbye, to loneliness and welcome in the newly created day. With a love that is destined too be, forever faithfully yours.

20.

Why do you giggle
19 Oct 2009

For Tommy and me, hell had come calling. The battle raged on and the screams of the wounded and dying, started to win over the reverb of the gun fire and explosions. Death had heard... and was here, it was hungry for flesh and new souls to own.

I remember it like yesterday, even though its been ten years since then. The guns were firing and the bullets were flying... and my friend was dying. His head laid in my lap, his blue eyes were slowly fading to gray, as he slowly slipped away. Into that great abyss of darkness, where we all must go some day.

My hands ached from the pain of trying to hold his stomach together, as his intestines kept seeping out. Looking for the freedom and space of the outside world. I could no longer tell the blood from the mud, that was collecting all around us. Pooling from the multiple wounds, my young and dear friend had sustained, that fateful day.

I had already used up all the readily available bandages, on the last soldier that had been hit by enemy bullets. He was alright, he would live. If only the helicopter would arrive in time, to transport Tommy back to station Bravo. Where the medics could give him better aid, bandage him with dressings I no longer had this day. Station Bravo was where the main medics stayed, waiting to help the hurt and dying. That seemed to pile up each and every day.

I could hear all around me "Doc over here. Man down, man down!". But still I held onto my youngest recruit, still I tried to keep his intestines inside his body. I could see in Tommy's eyes, that it wouldn't be long, before the ferry man would come calling for Tommy's spirit. And nothing I could do, would stop the black blood from oozing out of his chest and the ever growing pile of newly released intestines, from saying hello to the great angel of death.

Tommy was only nineteen, freshly from eleven bravo school. Home of the grunt soldier, the field dog, the soldier who went in first and came out last. I was the medic of his platoons, he was only a child and still looked at the world with the eyes of innocence and the knowledge that he could make a real change in the world.

In the intensity of battle its strange to say, that time can stand still, but at that very moment two things happened at once. The world became bright as the sun, and at the same time dark as the center of a black hole. And in that center of that black hole I saw him, the angel of death... the ferry man.

I tried with all my might to pick up Tommy's insides, and shove them back into his body, all the while trying to push my body back and through the rubble that was once, the wall to a families home. But still the image came closer to us, and in that split moment in time I wasn't fully sure if the angel of death was coming for Tommy, me or the both of us.

I was pulled out of my trance by a sound, the sound of giggling. Which I thought was Tommy gurgling, as the darkening blood started to seep out of the corners of his mouth. But it wasn't gurgling I heard, it was Tommy giggling and smiling that golden smile of youth. And the knowledge that he had done all he could have done, and that everything will be alright and not to fear the specter of death looming over us.

The shadow of death stood over Tommy and I for just a second, or was it longer, I do not know. His Stygian pits he used for eyes, stared at me for the longest time, gauging my soul and weighing all the things I've done and the things I should have done. This went on for how long I don't know, for in that very next drop in the sands of time, a great explosion exploded, no more then a hundred feet from where we rested. Tommy and I.

In that second the outside world crept back in and I could see the battle raging on again and I could see the grayness take hold over Tommy's blue eyes. He was gone, no more would I hear his giggles, no more would I see his golden smile ready and waiting for a new day.

I was a sergeant back then in my military days and I was a medic to a great bunch of guys, the dog soldiers, my comrades... my friends. But this was not my first job in the military, years ago I was an information collector of dirty secrets and dirty deeds. And in my youth I had lost my faith in my younger years, in my fellow man, in myself, before I became a medic. The truths of the world as and information collector had darkened my heart, with the pains of things I had done and things I seen and learned.

But now I wanted to give back, I wanted to become a medic and a nurse to help others and to make amends for what I've done and said in the past. But I was still dark in the my heart, that was until a simple child of nineteen, gave to me what I had lost in my youth. My giggles, my hopes and my faith in my fellow man.

I laid my friend down, picked myself up and ran. I ran all day and night, giving aid and a giggle to one and all that laid, screamed and prayed. For help and an end to the madness of hell, on the battlefield that day.

Years have passed since that fateful day and people ask me all the time, why do you giggle so much. I say nothing. Its for Tommy that I giggle. For all the moments he gave to me, in those short four months of knowing him. For the golden smile he gave to the world and the cheerful giggle that came so easily to his lips.

For giving me back my faith in the knowledge that if we give back, to all we do. It doesn't matter if we live short or long, or if we make a change or just try. What really matters is that we giggle and give a great big smile. Saying hello and welcome to one and all we see and send out our love to the morning, noon and evening breeze.

For one day the ferry man will come calling, and when you are standing at the feet of St Petters podium. It may be the giggles in life that we give out freely to the world, that he puts on the scale. Labeled Heaven or Hell, that will tip or fate. For a giggle held back becomes a stone in the pit of our stomach, weighing down our immortal soul. Tipping the scale too Hell!

So, I give a giggle each and every day. Till the giggles become easy and readily available without trying, to every one in every way. So when people ask me why I giggle, I say nothing. I just give then a giggle and a great big smile and remember my friend Tommy till the end of my days. See you soon Tommy, I hope and pray...

The End!

21.

The cultivating of a killer
11 Aug 2019

Effort takes time, like the growth of a sycamore tree. Tending to the soil, before the seed is planted. Giving time, for it to take root. Watching each centimeter of growth, as it reaches for the life giving light.

Watering the foundation, setting the pathway of its machinations too breast. As the branches are bound, to a preordained position. Following the creators design, unknowingly abiding by the rules pre-given.

Effort takes time, simple steps too a melody yet heard and yet harvested. The grower waits, developing the fruit of their labors. Waiting for the day of absolution.

When the soul becomes ripe, for tilling. And the creation is set loose, on an unexpected world. Perfection takes time, now the creator sits and waits, for the performance of a life time, to begin.

22.

Then there was you
20 March 2019

Endless days of patience, dwindling from one to the other, occupied my waking days and restless nights. Turning a quiet repose, too an unquenchable thirst.

Till you.

It wasn't one of those things you plan for, not even one you wish for, no it was far better. And more real then anything I've ever seen, known or done.

Because of you.

I now have a purpose. A laser focus, in an old passion. One neglected and placed to the wayside of doubt, but has resurfaced anew.

Because of you.

So, with a blossoming hunger, too refresh my creativity and strengthen my potential. I'll strive ever forward. Waiting for the day we meet.

Then there was you.

23.

Twelve years… and a day
28 July 2018

Time has flown by, in these last twelve years. Yet still I linger with the memories of you, and the pain of my youthful doings. Wishing to wright the wrongs of the past, and head into a brighter future.

Where the daemon's of my life, no longer tear at my inner soul and my unawakened mind. Twelve years I've searched for the pathways of redemption, patience and peace.

Only to find the makings, of a great wall of despair barring my way. Challenging me to climb out of hopelessness and woe, daring me to make a new start. Failing at every turn.

With twelve years of youth sliding away, twelve years of hope fading away, twelve years of loneliness choosing too stay. I linger in the house of past dreams and dreamscape's, sinking ever farther into the mouth of madness and willful destruction.

Twelve years have passed away and still I choose to stay, searching for the redemption of a future day. Praying I'll find the strength, to last another twelve years… and a day. Here in this home I've made.

24.

A Thanksgiving to remember
01 Dec 2007

Have you ever wondered how your first major holiday after a terrible divorce would go? Such as the all in cumbersome turkey day. Well, take a little journey with me and I'll give you my most memorable holiday yet.

It all started on the morning of thanksgiving, after getting off of work that morning, from working all night at the local hospital. After I got off I needed to stop off at the local grocery store, to pick up my duck and stuffing and all the other munchies and crunches one would get for a thanksgiving feast. As I've done for every thanksgivings I could remember after I got married.

I grew up in Hawaii and it was a local tradition to cook a duck instead of a turkey for most of my friends families. And to be honest duck is far tastier then turkey, in my opinion. So when I finally got the chance to cook my own thanksgiving meal, I wanted to do it the way I remembered my friends and their families having thanksgiving.

When I came home after the grocery store, max (my overly hyper boxer) and I played in the backyard for and hour or so, then I went back inside to start the thawing of the frozen duck in the sink and then went to bed. It was the end of a long three day shift at the hospital in the NICU (Neonatal Intensive Care Unit) as a nurse. I slept the entire day away. Now thats how you celebrate a major holiday, in bed... asleep. Oh what it gets better.

So max and I were once again playing out in the backyard again, its now midnight and the duck the duck has been cooking for nearly three hours. And it was starting to smell really good, I think it will be my best one yet. Being that it was nearly one in the morning, I decided to do something I've been putting off for some time now.

So, I'm nailing down my dogs carpet in his new dog house I built for him six months ago. What, what... I did say that I've been putting it off for a while now. Now in case you don't remember its a little past one in the morning of the night of thanksgiving. And I'm nailing carpet in my dogs dog house with a very large hammer. In order to get the full picture, you have to imagine a fairly large shoulder guy with his upper body in the dog house, and the rest of him lying on the back porch concrete floor.

Yes you heard me right, I was nailing down carpet in the middle of the night. Well this didn't sit well with my now extremely pissed off dog. I guess he thought I was taking over his territory or something, I mean the nerve of him, I built the dang thing after all I could do what I wanted with it... right.

So he decides to take his aggression out on the backyard and the multiple toys he loved to play with. So at some point this wasn't good enough for him and he decided to take a friendly nibble on my right calve. Scaring the holy you know what out of me.

So I did the only thing a strong and virile man as myself could do, I screamed and slammed my head on the ceiling of the dog house. Instantly I new something was wrong when a ungodly pain shot throughout my entire skull, with a small dribble of blood started to trickle down the side of my face.

Now I didn't know it was blood at the time, and being a nurse I instantly surmised that I had punctured my brain and I was leaking CSF fluid (cerebrospinal fluid). Now I know that I woke up at least on person in the neighborhood, what with the screaming in all. And if the first scream didn't wake up any of the neighbors, then the near destruction of my dogs dog house as I tried to get out. Then the yelling at my sweet boxer who was just playing would have, as I ran into the house and into the bathroom to look at the mirror and my head.

In my haste to look at my head, I had left the back door open (you'll want to remember this point in the story). I told you it gets better, and what has happened so far is nothing compared to what comes next. After a minute or two in front of the bathroom mirror, assessing what happened to my head. I came to the conclusion that I only punctured my head a millimeter or two, so I did the only thing a man in my position could do.

I ran to the back door, where my dog was sitting in the middle of the backyard, with one of those, oh snap expressions on his face. As I flew out the back door (still open) where I commenced to give my beloved boxer an old fashion smack down, and put some real hurt on my soon to be dead dog. So as I'm flying out the back door and giving my very large boxer a full on tackle any NFL pro player would be proud of. I'm imagining all manners of moves I'm going to put on him, and maybe even a bit or two to one of his ears. What, I gotta show him who's boss and put him in his place. Thats all I'm saying

Now before you all go and start screaming at me for animal abuse, my dog and I play like this all the time. And I'm not ashamed to say he wins most of the time. Max and I went back and forth me bitting him and him bitting me, well nibbling he was the best dog anyone could ever ask for. All the while I was trying to be the first person to make a dog pretzel out of him. It wasn't in his nature to really bit anyone, and it wasn't in my nature to really hurt my best friend.

After forty five minutes or so of wrestling with my dog, my adrenalin and Max's energy was spent so we went inside to have our thanksgiving dinner. It's now a little after three in the morning and I'm a mess and max is still looking like he just came out of the dog salon. And I'll have you know the duck came out perfect. So you would think that this would be the end of my story, and you would be right if it were anybody else but me. Nope, it wasn't.

So I go back to work that next Friday night, with a new wound and a funny little story to tell my coworkers, too the enjoyment of all. I mean come on, they didn't have to laugh that long, sheesh. After another busy three days, its Monday morning and I'm ready for a warm fire, some good wine, a good book to read and my lovable dog by my side.

When I get home Max's is outside eating his morning meal, so I decide to go and sit down on my old recliner chair. When out of the corner of my eye I see something dart past my sofa with a squeak. Yep thats right, I said a squeak. I quickly jumped up, grabbed my old military flash light and flashed its beam behind the sofa. Where to my surprise, I see a trail of dog food and mouse droppings. Oh snap and yuck, is all I can get out of my now hanging on the sofa bottom jaw.

Now max and I, who I let in to track down that mouse, spent the next two hours tearing the living room apart looking for that little pest. And after two hours and no mouse found I decided to clean up all the mess (it should be noted at this time in the story that my vacuum cleaner had decided to call it quits, yep right after Black Friday, did I say I have the worst luck in the world.). This is of special importance to all the Black Friday shoppers, they will fill my pain. Now back to the story.

Being the manly guy that I am, I refused to go to the store and buy a new one, so I used my garage shop vac. What, I'm a guy after all. Sheesh. If you've never used a shop vac before, let me give you a mental image of what they look like. They are round with wheels and a long hose to suck with at the end there is little and I mean little brush to suck things up with. Its now an hour later when the living room floor is completely clean, and all the furniture is placed back in its original spot.

The fire I had started when I came home is now a little flame and the wine was accidentally dumped into the sink. What, I don't know how the wine got into the sink, it was probably that dame mouse. So I grabbed the only thing left, my book and sat in my chair once again, hopping to calm down and start the beginning of a four day vacation. When I hear scratch, scratch squeak and some more scratching coming from the kitchen.

Max looks at me with his stubby little tail wagging a mile a minute thinking its play time again, all the while looking at me as to say, its go time daddy and took off to the kitchen. With me following behind that silly dog of mine thinking, am I ever going to get to start my new book and who dumped my wine in the dame sink.

I could hear the mouse and it had made its way behind my over size refrigerator. Oh great, now what do I do? The only thing I could do, I pulled the refrigerator out a little and looked behind it to see if I could find that dame mouse. It was sitting about a foot up and in a little hole in the wall that the plumbers make to place the water line hookup in. The mouse was attempting to chew its way threw the plastic box, which I guess was its attempt to reach the inside of the wall and a speedy get-a-way.

After a few minutes of soft cursing and jumping up and down in the kitchen. I looked at max and gave him the order to watch the left flank while I grabbed my tiki torch that I had just bought two weeks ago. Now with the flash lite in my mouth and the tiki torch held like a spear. I jabbed for the unwanted intruder with my great and manly skills. With probably more luck then anything, I was able to knock this unwanted holiday visitor off the perch. Where he fell to the kitchen floor, knocked out stone cold, but unharmed.

So after a few minutes of arguing with max, as to who was going to go behind the refrigerator and pick up the little fellow. He decided to give me one of his famous looks, it's your house dude and immediately walked back to his over sized blue pillow for a morning nap.

Not wanting a reunion on Christmas day, I picked up the little guy and placed him into a shoe box with some holes in the top and the sides for air. Then I grabbed my coat an took the little fellow out to the woods in the hill country. Letting him go with a giggle and a smile. Giving him a holiday suggestion as he woke up and made his way out of the shoe box. Telling him to go and visit his relatives in another neighborhood next thanksgiving or maybe the noisy neighbor down the street. Now that would be sweet justice, right.

As I watched him or her, never really knowing which it was, I smiled to myself and hummed a little tune. Knowing this will go down for me at least, as one of the weirdest holidays max and I could ever have.

Happy holidays to you and yours and everyone else this holiday season, please be safe and give everyone you meet a smile and a giggle.

The End!

25.

The measure of a life
16 July 2018

When the bell tolls, what will be the measure of my life… exemption or expulsion?

Will it be a man who challenged the very nature of life, or stood for purity of ones beliefs? Or will the slate of my existence be nothing more then a brick of failure after failures?

At the end, when the final beat of a lonely souls cadence is silenced. Will the scale be kind or will the gavel of eternity swing with a reckoning of damnation?

Sealing a pathway of redemption and resolution, from an unworthy human, not worth requital. Or will the final gong bring everlasting peace-love-hope, to a weary soul…

Bang. Bang. Goes the gavel.

26.

The gift of a kiss
21 Sept 2017

Note: there are two different styles for this one.

-Style one-

Days may be good
Days may be bad

Don't worry little one
Here's a kiss, my little angel

It's a gift left on a wish
That I leave, on your cheek tonight

For when days are bad
Remember little one

Daddy, left you a gift
Of a kiss with a wish

That you'll be safe, forever more
Starting this, wet and stormy night.

-Style two-

When the sins of the mother and father, send ripples through the eternal night, of have and have not. Remember my sweet angel, it's a gift left on a wish, that I leave for you this night. In the blessing of a simple little kiss, on your cheek this wet and stormy night.

Don't you worry my little angel, good days will come and bads will go. The sins of the father and mother may make it fall tears, like sheets of rain that darken your light. But it's this gift of a kiss, that will release a wish. That will take away, the rainy days and stormy nights.

Expelling, all your worries and fright. For the sins of the mother and father, shall never visit you again, in the dead of night. Here's a kiss my angel, its a gift of a wish, that will set you free. From this fright in the darkest part, of your eternal light.

27.

The looking glass
25 Sept 2019

What makes a person who they are or are not? Is it the very essence of what they will become or become not? Is it the moments of triumphs. Or the ones of trials failed, that defines the very core of their being? Placing them on the path they are destined to tread. For good or for bad?

If in knowing that the act of what you did or didn't do, set the foundation of your future. Would you be strong enough, too look through the looking glass of possibilities? Seeing all the realities, you could of had, might of had if you only did things differently.

Knowing, that the one you're living now, was the wrong choice. Could you be that strong? Would you have the courage, to continue on the path that lies before you, knowing what might might have been?

Could you?

28.

Eternal Struggle... Become more then you are
27 March 2017

Desperation is the secret, of times futility.
In the very nature of finding one's future.
While pondering, the very essence and existence
of one's self worth. In the measurement of self
awareness and faith.

In the hope that only expectations of an outcome,
can drown the perpetual motion, of the emptiness of self
realization. In all things learned and forgotten,
loved and lost.

Only by tossing aside, all mental and material
possessions of self worth and want. Can you dispel
the falseness of times constraints and constant distraction's.

In the endeavors to build your inner soul, to match
your outer desires. You only confound your path of
enlightenment and innocence growth. Forging an
outer shell of false illusion's.

Befuddling all possibilities, of everlasting knowledge
and spiritual nurturing. In the attaining, of inner and
outer

peace. Of one's own self worth and developmental respect of one's own being.

The pathways of enlightenment, are estranged for all who walk the road of inner and outer peace. Granting only glimpses, of times grand design. In the eternal struggle, to become more then you are.

29.

We...
17 March 2012

We judge, before we see
we condemn, before we hear
we pain, before we feel
and... we hold
when we should, **forgive**.

Note to readers: This is a different poem I called, We.

We
19 September 2019

We is, as we are
We are, as we were
We were, as we will be
We be... as we are.

30.

How can, how many, how does
01 Jan 2012

How can I be so alive, yet feel so dead?
How can I live a life, yet walk in dread?

A rose will bloom, and soon fade
So does… a youth… so does the fairest maid.

How many lives will it take, to wash away my vile wake?
How many paths shall I destroy, to seal my fate?

A rose will bloom, and soon fade
So does… a youth… so does the fairest maid.

How does one say… the sorries, in life's mistakes?
How does one change, the remaining
of his everlasting days?

A rose will bloom, and soon fade
So does… a youth… so does the fairest of maids.

31.

Its going to be a great day... or not
30 August 2019

Note to the readers: This little micro story was created for a writing site I belong too. The challenge was to come up with a short story about an inanimate object and that object would see, feel and even speak to other inanimate objects. So even though it may seem strange, I hope you will enjoy the journey, as I had in creating it.

****

The new day started off with a jingle at the back door of the little corner store. By all standards it was a simple store, with simple little things. But today was delivery day and anything could happen on delivery day.

The old shopkeeper looked down at Sally, his ten year old boxer. All the while making his way to the back door, where the jingling was coming from. "I'm coming. I'm coming, give an old man a minute or two to get to the blasted door. Dash it all," said the old shopkeeper as she walked into the storage room, in the back of his shop.

He wasn't a mean man by any means, but today was his least favorite day of the month. Delivery day. "Hump! I hate delivery day. I'm getting to old for this stuff Sally old girl," said the shopkeeper as he looked down, to the only friend he had left in the world.

Sally was all he had left, and being ten, he didn't know how much longer he would have left with her. She was his best friend, the best friend he'd ever had. That is if anyone ever took the time to ask him. He was a simple man and owned and ran a simple little shop. Staying out of peoples way and asking the same to one and all. Except Sally of course.

"What do you say old girl," said the shopkeeper to Sally. "Want to bite the delivery guy for me this morning?"

This brought out a laugh from the old shopkeeper and a large snort from Sally, as he opened the storage rooms back door. "Don't even think about it Sally, or I will stop bringing you extra treats. You know the ones with the tasty center, you love so much," said the young and pretty delivery driver.

As the back door opened up and she saw Sally wagging her stubby excuse for a tail. And the old shopkeeper with his sour puss, grumpy old face all twisted up in a knot. "Up to your old tricks again I see. You should be ashamed of yourself, trying to get Sally to take a chomp out of me, you old fool. You should know by now, that us girls stick together. Isn't that right Sally old girl?"

Sally just sat there waiting patiently for her treat, that she knew was coming. She just had to wait for her owner to turn around and grab the clipboard, he kept hanging on the wall behind the back door. The old shopkeeper knew that the delivery driver, would sneak treats to her when he wasn't looking. But he didn't mind, Sally was getting older and she deserved and extra treat or two now and then.

He wouldn't admit it, but he liked the new delivery driver. He could tell she was a dog person by nature. That's why he always took a little more time, in finding his clipboard. It was a game they played, him and the pretty delivery driver. If he was pressed to admit it, he counted her as a dear friend. But he would never tell her that. After all, an old man did have his pride.

It was on this day that the shop was due, for a few new items to be added to the inventory of the little shop. A few new dog and cat toys, along with this seasons new winter cloths. It was supposed to be an extra cold winter this year, from what the weatherman kept saying on the evening news. She he took a chance and ordered some extra boxes, hoping to make a profit this winter season.

It wasn't until after all the boxes were dropped off and the delivery driver was well on her way. That he noticed and additional box to his original order. "Well, what do we have here, old girl," said the shopkeeper to Sally. "Seems we got an extra package. What do you think, should we take a peek inside to see what's in there?"

Now unbeknownst to the shopkeeper and Sally, the box was full of a new type of toy. One that would be a big hit with dog and cat owners all over the world.

****

The little toy wasn't sure what was going on, what with being just born two days ago. But what it did know, was that it had to get out of this stuffy dark box thingy. The other guys in there were getting on its nerves and giving it a headache. They just wouldn't shut up, it was nonstop.

From the first moment he could remember. They just kept on asking question after question. Like, what is this place and what was the belt looking thingy we road on. And why are they putting us in plastic bags, and just what the heck is that cardboard box thing doing at the end of this belt thingy.

They just kept going on, and on, and on... Question after question after question. But finally the box was open and the first rays of daylight graced its face, since its creation just two days ago. He wasn't sure, but it had felt like more then just two days had gone by. It felt like eternity had gone by, especially being crammed in that smelly box with all the other toys like him.

But with the opening of the box, the little toy got its first look at its new world. And the toy just knew it was meant for something very special. It just knew it. The little toy just knew, that he was meant for something great, he felt it throughout his little rubber body.

It didn't take long before he was pulled out of the cardboard box, then placed into a metal bin and put on a metal shelf. In what looked to be a small and simple little shop of some kind. Now he wasn't sure, but the toy thought that the place must be an animal store of some kind. He could see all kinds of other plastic and rubber toys, and he could hear strange sounds, coming from around the corner at the end of the isle.

The little toy kept looking around the shop as best as he could, he wiggled this way and tried to move that way. All the while trying to get a better idea, of just where he was. The toys next to him just kept on asking the same questions. Like, what is this new thingy were in and why are we all crammed together and what kind of place is this anyways? The little rubber toy just knew, that if he didn't get out of this metal bin he was going to go crazy, if he didn't get placed into another location far, far away from these other toys.

No sooner said then done, the little toy was picked up by the old shopkeeper and was taken to the rear of the store. As he was being transfered to a new location, he could see he was right it was a pet store of some kind. He could see all kinds of things, from other toys to cloths and even different types of animals, like dogs and cats.

There were strange things in glass tanks swimming around in water, and even some in cages that had wings. How strange he thought, why would someone put an animal with wings in a little cage like that. It didn't seem right to him some how, after all aren't creatures with wings supposed to be free so they can fly around in the open sky.

The little toy didn't have much time to ponder the answer to his question. Because the old shopkeeper had came up to a old large wooden desk, where he set the little toy down on the counter top of the desk. The little toy wasn't sure what was happening, and he was scared. A new sensation to be sure, one the little toy didn't like at all. The toy was taken out of the plastic bag and was then placed inside a glass box under the top of the wooden desk in the back of the pet shop.

There was all kinds of other things inside the glass box. The little toy saw different types of toys and clothes, why even food in plastic bags. The toy saw a sign taped to the inside of the glass box, but he couldn't make out what was written on the other side of the sign. "I wonder what is written on that sign in front of us," thought the little toy.

"Hay, can you tell me what's written on the other side of that sign in front of us," said the little toy. "I can't see it from here." Asked the little toy to the small bag of puppy chew treats next to him.

The small bag of puppy chew treats, looked at the new toy and said "demo items. Not for sale."

"Demo items. Not for sale. What does that mean?" asked the little toy.

"It means that we are stuck in here for the people, who come into the store to see," said the bag of chew treats. "But we are not to be bought, we are only to be looked at. The items on the metal shelves are the ones who get bought. They are the ones who get to leave this store. While we just site here in this display case all day and night, never to be purchased and never to be used for the purpose we were made for."

This brought on a strange thought to the little toys brain. "But I know I'm special. I know that I'm meant to do important and wonderful things," said the little toy. "How am I going to accomplish that, if I'm not for sale? How will I find my place in this world and a meaning to my life, if the sign says demo only, not for sale?"

****

The shopkeeper picked up the box and set it on his work table, then went to find his box cutter. "Where is that blasted box cutter," said the old shopkeeper. "Sally did you take the dang box cutters again?" Sally just snorted again, all the while giving her owner one of her famous looks. "Don't you go blaming this on me you old crazy fool," thought Sally as she made her way to the water bowl in the corner of the storage room.

Sally knew her owner liked to blame things going missing on her, she didn't mind, not really. But she would sure as heck give him a dirty look or two, for blaming her for whatever item he misplaced and went missing. Sally gave her owner this look for two reasons. One to let him know it wasn't she, who misplaced what ever he was looking for and second to make him smile and laugh his head off.

If anyone ever took the time to ask her, she would have to admit that she didn't mind being accused of taking stuff. Because she could give her owner one of her looks and make her owner smile and laugh. Sally knew she was the only thing left in this world, that the shopkeeper cared about.

She also knew he had little joy left in his old life, especially after his wife of fifty years passed away just one year ago today. So Sally didn't mind being blamed now and then, not if she could make him laugh. Every once in a while, he was a good man and a hard worker and most of all a good owner to Sally. It was Sally's job after all, to bring happiness to his life. It was what she was born for and what she was meant to do.

****

Weeks went by and the little toy just sat there, in the glass box just looking out into the strange new world it had been brought into. All the while watching other things, being bought and sold to all manner of people. The little toy wondered when it would be its turn, to be bought and sold.

Still, the little toy did enjoy watching all the people and seeing what they brought up to the old wooden counter. Where the old shopkeeper and his dog, sat patiently for people to come in and buy something. He especially liked it when the strange people, brought their pets with them, he liked to see all the crazy cloths and haircuts they had on them.

"Spike, spike. Hay spike, look at this one. It has some kind of strange fur growing on its body, but it only has the hair in spots and there round," said the little toy to the spiked dog collar. "How strange, I've never seen one like this before."

"Thats because its a poodle, and its hair doesn't grow like that," said the leather dog collar, all covered with shiny metal spikes. "Its the poodles owner that has its hair cut like that, they think it looks cool or something. From what I've heard those dogs hate it, especially the boy dogs."

"Well, I think it looks stupid. How is the poor dog going to stay warm, what with all that cold wind blowing out there" said the little toy.

"You silly block head. Owners don't have time to care about their pets," said Spike. "They just want to look good, while they are walking their dogs outside for all the world to see. Now please leave me alone, I was dreaming of being sold to a nice couple with a lady boxer."

It didn't take long for all of the other little toys like him to be sold off, now he was the only one left. The little toy wondered where they were going to and what was waiting for them when they got there. As the little toy looked through the shops front window, he could see the sun was setting and new that the old shopkeeper and his dog would be closing up the pet store soon.

As he looked at the front window, he was sure that he was destined to remain behind this glass case. To never be sold to a loving owner of some pet and never to find his true purpose in this life. "I don't know how much longer I can stand being here, knowing all the other ones like me have found their place and purpose in this world." Said the little toy to know one in particular. The little toy was feeling about as low as a rubber toy could feel.

And thats when it happened. The lights were turned off and the old shopkeeper and his dog walked to the side door, the one that lead upstairs to the small apartment that they called home. The little toy watched as the door was opened and the old dog started to make its way up the rickety old stairs. The ones he could hear creaking and cracking every morning and night when they went up and down.

But something was different this time, the old man stopped and said to Sally. "Its been a busy day Sally old girl, how about we have some fun. What do you say." The little toy heard the old shopkeeper and wondered what was going on, they never stopped at the door. They always opened the door and made their way upstairs, but today they just stood there looking at each other.

"Spike. Hay Spike, something strange is going on," said the little toy. "Now that old shopkeeper and his dog are just standing at their apartment door. What do you think they're up too?"

"Its nothing. He probably just forgot something, you wait and see," said Spike. "Just watch, he will come back over here and get what ever he forgot and then he will go back to the door and make his way upstairs for the night. Now leave me alone, I want to get some sleep before the start of a new day and more stupid questions from you."

But he wasn't so sure, this felt different to the little toy. Thats when he saw the old man turned around and look right at him, with a strange little smile on his wrinkly old face. As he made his way to the new little rubber toy, they got in a few weeks ago.

"Spike. Hay Spike, that old man is looking at me funny," said the little rubber toy. "I don't think I like the way he's looking at me. You don't think he's coming over here to throw me away, now that I'm the last one here like me, do you Spike?"

"If he does, it will be a blessed day." Said Spike as he tried to shift his position and hopefully get back to sleep, again.

The little toy looked over to his only friend. "I'm sure that he's not going to do that, besides you would miss me if I was gone. Right Spike? Spike." The little toy looked again to his friend, but Spike had turned over and didn't say anything back.

Thats when the door to the glass case opened up and the old shopkeeper reached inside to grab hold of the little rubber toy and took it out of the demo case only box. The old shopkeeper then closed the back door to the demo case and started back to the side door. The one that lead up to the little apartment that the old man and his dog called home.

****

The little toy was excited and scared at the same time. This was something new, he was going somewhere else and anywhere else had to be a good thing, thought the little toy. "This has to be a good right? I mean if he was going to throw me away, he could of just thrown me into the trash bin right next to the glass case. Right?" thought the little toy.

The door to the apartment where the two of them lived was opened and the little toy could see all kinds of new things, it had never seen before. He watched Sally run into the apartment and then jump up on an old looking sofa. Then the toy heard the old shopkeeper saying something to Sally, but couldn't quite make out what he had said.

"Dang it what did that old man say to his dog. I couldn't hear him, not with his dirty old hands covering up my ears." Said the little toy out loud, to know one in particular. "Hay. Old man, where are you taking me? If you're going to throw me out, why didn't you do it back downstairs in the shop?"

The toy watched as the old shopkeeper reached into this cold box, then he saw the old man bring something out with his hands. Thats when the old shopkeeper closed the metal door and walk to a new type of counter top, placing both the little toy and the cold item from the cold box on top of this new metal counter top. All the while saying "I got a surprise for you Sally, one that you'll just love."

"Hay, old man. Can you hear me, what's going on?" asked the little toy sitting on the metal counter top. It was then that the old man turned around with a knife in his wrinkly old hand and smiled to the little toy with an even wrinklier old face.

The old shopkeeper grabbed the new toy and used the knife to cut into the plastic bag that was covering the new toy and take out the little rubber toy. He then used the knife to cut open the small bag of chewy treats, he kept in the refrigerator for Sally. It was then that the little toy became very nervous and scared. This was a new feeling for the little toy and he didn't like how it made him feel.

"Hay, hay... I said HAY! What are you doing now old man... no, no! Don't stick that there, thats not an inny. Its an outty.

Ouch! Hay, just what do you think your doing with that?" said the little toy, as a whole new set of feelings where happening all at once to him.

At the same moment that the little toy was having a life altering moment with the shopkeeper. Sally got her first smell of one of her favorite chewy treats, dropping the old stuff hear she loved to naw on. Sally made her way to the kitchen, she could she her owner messing around with one of those new toys. The ones that came a couple of weeks ago, but she didn't understand why he was putting her chewy treat inside of it.

"Ok. Lets have a little chat, what do you say old man? If you stop doing what your doing right now, this won't get ugly. Hay old man, can you hear me?" said the little toy as the old man finished stuffing in the last of the chewy treats, he could fit into the inside of the little rubber chew toy.

Sally couldn't take it 5 any longer, she had to know what her owner was doing and why he was putting in her second favorite thing to eat, inside of that new toy thingy. Sally got up on her back legs and placed her front paws onto the edge of the kitchen counter top.

"Sally, no girl get down. You'll find out what I have for you in just a moment, old girl," said the old shopkeeper. "You need to learn some patients after all." The shopkeeper put the bag of chewy treats back into the refrigerator and made his way to the little living room where they spent most of their time in, when not downstairs tending to the pet store.

"I think you broke something inside of me old man," said the little toy, who was now full of dog chewy treats. "Hay old man... I don't feel so good, what did you put inside of my?"

The old shopkeeper sat down into his favorite old reclining chair and turned on the small TV. It was an old TV from the eighties. Sally followed her owner around to the front of the chair and sat down on the old green shag rug, also from the eighties and waited for her owner to drop that new toy thingy that smelled so yummy.

The old shopkeeper just sat there for a moment or two to watch Sally and to see if she was going to stay there or make a break for the toy in his right hand. After a few more seconds the old shopkeeper couldn't take it any more, and just had to give the new surprise too her.

"Here you go Sally old girl," said her owner. "Its a new toy, one that I bet your going to just love." The shopkeeper tossed the little toy onto the ground in front of Sally. Laughing as he stared intently at his beloved boxer, wondering what she was going to do first and what she was going to make of this strange new chew toy, that he had just filled with one of her favorite chew treats.

The little toy sailed through the air, then bounced a couple of times on the green shag carpet, coming to rest just under Sally's big wet nose. "Oh, really. You take me out of the glass case, then you assault me with some strange thing. Cold might I add and then you stick something into my...," said the little toy. "And then you have the nerve to toss me onto the ground like some unwanted piece of trash. You'll be hearing from my lawyer old man."

It was then that the little toy felt something cold, wet and hard take hold of its rubber body. "What's happening now?" said the little toy, as Sally picked up the new toy and started to pick at the treats inside of her new favorite chew toy. "Hay now dog, put me down. Oh no you didn't, you slobbering mutt."

"Didn't you hear me dog, I said stop that this instant!"

"What are you doing now... no, no, no."

"That's not where you stick your tongue. And, hay! What

are you doing with that cold wet nose of yours?" said the little toy, all the while seeing and hearing the old man laughing his wrinkly old head off. This went on for some time, Sally doing her best to get at all of the chewy treats inside of the little toy. And the little toy spewing out a litany of curses, that would make a seasoned sailor blush from head to toe.

****

"What do you think of the new toy Sally?" said the old shopkeeper. "It looks like will have all kinds of fun this winter, with this little guy... right." But Sally didn't even hear him, she was having the time of her life, ripping into this new toy thingy too even stop and look up at her owner. Who couldn't stop laughing at seeing her having so much fun.

"So good. How is this so good?" thought Sally.

"Fun, does this look like fun to you man?" said the little rubber chew toy. "I'm being molested by a furry beast of an animal."

Then the little toy saw the face of Sally and heard the laughter coming from the old shopkeeper. The little toy saw the happiness, that came with the playful antics of the slobbering mutt. And her attempt at getting to all of the food, the old shopkeeper placed inside of it. The little toy knew in that instant, it had found its reason for being and it had found its place where it belonged.

The old shopkeeper couldn't remember the last time he had so much fun, watching his beloved boxer tearing into a chew toy. He leaned back into his old recliner chair and just sat there enjoying the moment. Then a thought came to him.

"Hay Sally, what do you think about putting something new into your little toy tomorrow?" said the shopkeeper, as he leaned forward to see if she would stop what she was doing and take a second to look up at him. "How about we put some Spam in there, I bet you'll go nuts for some Spam. It's your favorite treat... right Sally?"

Sally didn't even take a second to think about it, and didn't need to be asked twice. When she heard the word Spam, she dropped her new chew toy and jumped up and started looking around for her most favorite treat in the world. Seeing no Spam anywhere in site, Sally walked over to her owner and placed one very large paw on her owners right foot. All the while placing nearly all of her body weight down upon her owner foot.

"Hay now, Sally dear. I was just saying how about we place some of your favorite food in our new toy tomorrow," said the shopkeeper as he tried to pull his foot out from under his eighty five pound boxers front paw. "I never said today I would put some in there today Sally dear."

Sally leaned in a little further and just kept staring at her owner, for a few seconds longer. Then she snorted and went back to her new toy, attempting to get every last speck of food out of it. Thinking all the while, that if he didn't give her some Spam tomorrow, she just might not take her paw off of his foot so soon next time.

At just the exact same moment that Sally sat down and started back on her new chew toy, the can of Spam in the wooden cub board in the kitchen. Felt a chill climbing up its spin, all the while thinking to its self. "I have a very bad feeling, that its going to be a very bad day tomorrow. Yep, I just know its not going to be a good day."

The End

32.

She runs from her shame
24 Feb 2009

She walks at times, among the people of the world. Taking in all that's seen and felt, she guards her pain with ticks, pricks and stains.

She sits at times. Among the moving world above her, around her, till an involuntary movement, word or action. Gives those closest to her, a reason to complain. Her ticks.

She huddles at times. Among the dirty bins and alleyways. Home to pusher's, user's and needle filled bins, taking away her pains. Her pricks.

She hides at times. Among those who see her everyday, covering her body with filthy clothes. Rank with lice and mold, distracting all, to the emptiness that remains and the tears that drain. Her stains.

She walks, sits, huddles and hides among the homeless, running from the crash that took her family away. Because she hurried, worried and forgot to make them buckle their seat belts that fateful day. Losing her daughter, husband and son, when she rushed to get home. To her champagne.

She was attempting to cross the railroad track. Ignoring the lights, bars and horns wanting nothing more then to stop the complaining, fighting and noise. She crossed into the trains domain. Now she runs from her shame. Wrapping herself, in the past and her ever growing mental chains. Swearing to never again, drink champagne.

33.

The three seasons of a so called friendship
27 Jan 2011

Sweet beginnings. Rage with passion
with pleasure, with understanding.
That the hope will grow, friendship will bud
and one will become... known.

Blossomed middles. Burn with desire
with dreams, with attachment.
That all will be as one, friendship will last
and become... everlasting.

Sour endings. Linger in your mouth
in your soul, in your inner home.
That in giving yourself freely, friendship was a lie.
So once again, you forward to... another.

Endeavoring, to try again
A single soul, ply's the rivers of chance.
Fishing, for connections of trust
Instead of finding, heartbreak and rust.

34.

An Ode:
To the Crown, that is and is not hair
18 March 2010

Hair is the crown, that covers a weary head
whether it be straight, curled, short or long...
glory be, to those who's head is full, full of fear and woe.

For in their worry, they find solace
for in their sadness, they find peace
for in their loss... they find comfort.

In the glory that is hair. While tired fingers find joy
in the rhythmic movement, of lost thoughts,
of a lost way. All the while fingers twirl, seeking answers.

To a question... yet asked, yet known
to the mysteries of life, loss, faith, love.
And, as the every growing strands of hair, flows.

So too, will the trails of man, come to be known.
So grab that hair, glide that hand, and give a tug
when you've forgotten... where in
life you stand and have stood.

And as the last strands of hair falls,
and leave your weary head.
Forget not, even as the sun shines

down, on your bald head.
That with or without... your still
a strong and confident man.

35.

Acquiescing your fate
27 Nov 2010

Do you believe in the possibility, of the true spirit of your life's soul mate? That mirror image of your inner star, the outer breath of your world. Now if you believe in that, take a mental slip on the thought of your soul's desire.

Actually breathing the same air in your life span. Mind numbing in its purist form. For if its true, how long would it take to meet, to know, to have and to hold?

But... what if your days of living were years, even decades apart. Could you wait, spending the reincarnation of multiple lives, dancing the tune of patience and chastity... could you, should *you*?

Then compound that thought, with the unbelievable idea of that mirror image, of your inner hearts desire. Actually finding you.

Walking the roaming world of chance and fate, waiting for that moment to burst into your consciousness. Coming to know, in that very first inhalation, those unmeasurable short and unfathomably brief seconds of knowledge.

Giving life... to instantaneous connections becoming

real. Singing to all of creation that this is the one, that magical vision of purity. That spells the start, to the rest of your unworthy immortal life.

For meeting your soul's mate is worth a dream of infinite wishes. On a very short list of would be's and could be's. That sends the very core of a mind spinning, breathing worlds of hope and belief.

Spelling joy, and splendor on your face... for all the worlds of creation to no-longer believe... in disbelief. That thy own soul's truest mate has stepped up to the plate, giving fullness to your life, your fate.

Then fates bill comes crashing onto your reality. Spelling the doom of your destiny and giving pain to your exhalation. That timing is everything, that the movements and moments of one, collide in connection but rebound in the realization, of miss direction of paths.

For the mirror image of your inner being, is dating-married to a full and loving soul... even if its not the inner mirror of his or her own. Would it be right and true, to acquiesce the blinding image of what lies before you... should you, would *you*?

Could you be that honorable soul, to once again ride the time line of hope and faith? That one day it will be your home, that he or she will call to and say...

My purest soul. Stop your eternal roam, for destiny has finally found you. Willing all to see and know. That never again will the fates set your sails, to the emptiness of the universes unloving and uncaring home.

Because, we two stars of the same heaven, have finally found one and another. Now, we shine for everyone to see. Letting all believers of hopes love, relish in the knowledge.

That we all have a soul's inner and outer mate. That if everyone continues to harvest faith and believe... then yours too will find thee. As mine did to me.

36.

Hollow Resolve
24 Aug 2013

We were once soldiers. Holding ground not of this earth, but of our very souls. Taking lives came willingly. Giving, deaths release to all who crossed our path. Challenging all... who dared to take the reserve of our faith, or power. In the knowledge, that we were true to the cause, true to the plight and true to the outcome of our missions.

We were once soldiers. Who shed blood, pain and the steel of our fortitude. Of our resolutions in the truth of our cause. Challenging all... to judge our actions, our purpose of dominance. In knowing we were right, we were justified in the taking of lives, in the causing of suffering and the sterilization of their future. To any and all who would walk the pathways of corruption, indifference and decadence to their fellow man.

We were once soldiers. Who've grown indifferent to our present, from actions of our depleting youth, through acts of our past aggressions. Now decrepit of mind, lost in our soul and trodden in our hope. We float in our daily chores, giving no reprieve to what was lost. By heavy hand and ease of fingure, to those who gave rise to our nation's call.

We were once soldiers. Floating down the streets of our making, taking solace in the resolve that what we have done... is hollow. In all but one. For all who were soldiers, and carried the gun. Will be judged by all and forgiven by none. Because to take a life, whether for good or evil must never be done. For in the end all will be judged, by his most holy of perfect sons.

For we should have been growing faith, culturing love's resolve and giving help to one and all. By using our brains and hearts... not taking up guns, spreading hate and pain. For in doing so, we kill you-them-me and doom us all.

37.

Loves a bullet
25 March 2009

Every atom of her essence cries out to be held. Come to me, love me, be with me. Her eye's say what is and what I so want. She gives off all the signals of wanting, needing, hoping for the closeness that we both so need. But... there is pain. I misunderstood in the speed of the heart, and didn't match the expectancy of the mind.

One wanted to go forward slowly, the other at the speed of the shooters bullet. Now a bridge has been crossed into uncomfortable lands and the road back is laid with mines of distrust and hurt. Silence is left on the table of hope, with a side of discomfort resting on the taste buds of both of them.

He knew at an instant, that his bullet of love was too soon, to fast at offending and making her uncomfortable. So he let days of silence, turn into months of regret. Building a wall between... between two, that were meant to be one. Soul mates, lovers from the past. Each needing, wanting to create a new, warm and bright future.

They say only time can and will heal all wounds, but if its at the speed of the one and not the shooter. Then love will never become the seed of growth. It will stay in the ground and be forever at the ready, waiting for the future that will never come. For the slow bullet may eventually get to its intended target, but the receiver may have moved on.

So the shooter tries to rebuild the roadways of the heart, with slow intentions and smiles. Giving her time to except, know and come to see his own eyes of hope, love and the true feeling of his inner heart. Forever waiting patiently, for the moment to send out his next bullet of love, hoping and praying it will be received with a longing, willing and loving heart.

38.

The Crucible
13 Oct 2013

Childishness
of wonderment, on all things pleasurable.

Gathered
into every waking moment,
of tactile consciousness.

Indulgence
of all humanly desires,
bordering on the boundaries of apathy.

Withering
in the hollowness of absolution
in one's own actions.

Spiraling
into damnation, well over the precipice
of plausible control.

Falling
into the bowels, of self-incrimination
of complete decadence.

Realization
only through the purgatory,
of the mental crucible of one's own guilt.

Salvation

in atonement of all waking sin's
being mentally and spiritually achieved.

39.

Over Weight
09 Oct 2019

I walk in and the faint sounds of moo
hits my ears, inside I cry
as I sit down, one thought
takes control, chew-chew...

And chew some more
a size, that frightens the eye
obesity, some say
so heavy, that snails pass you by.

Conference time comes
talk-talk, so much talking
when is the food trolley, coming by
smell-sniff, yes... oh god yes.

It must be, has to be
food-food, the sustenance, I so need
platters come, platers go
rumble-grumble and rumble some more.

Hope my platters on the way
if not, I'll have to say
good bye and good day
this is sweet goodbye.

Because, I'm on my way
to the ever calling
oriental Noodle pot
at Safeway's!!!

40.

Risking All
09 Oct 2019

Just the two of us
setting footsteps down
upon strange lands
never knowing
where they go
denying passions felt
and never shown.

A whirlwind of creativity
at hand
all that's needed
is too
let go of past-future
and present.

Just join
one to the other
the other to all
then forever be two
who complete
creativity, in risking all.

41.

Love's golden years
07 April 2010

In the youth of the young
love, is vivacious and all consuming.
In our youthful years
we throw… each other and love away.

In the middle age of man and woman
love, is confusing-cumbersome.
In our middle years
we tear… each other and our love apart.

In the evaporating days of life
love, is feared second only to loneliness.
In our golden years
we pray… for the other, for love, instead of tears.

If only, in our youth
if only, in our middle
if only, in all our ages
we… could be of, be in, our golden years.

42.

Hack into life
20 Feb 2019

Tap tap
pitter patter
of little fingers
searching for one home.

in the heavenly keyhole
rounding second base
with intentions of fame
we play the ever growing.

All so knowing
iceberg of life, iceberg of change
freezing form shame
crying from constant pain.

Fingers go pitter pat
tap tap
ripy pity rap
for as long, as there's a game.

I will for ever hack
Into life's joys of pain
and get on with, what the
blue green, ball of life.

Has to throw at me
for no matter
where I go
into insanity or shame.

I will always remember
that to be truly free
all we have to do
is Hack into life.

Play the game...
so give me what you got
and I will do the same
year after year!!!

43.

The transformation
27 Oct 2009

A family ripped apart.
From the rage of a war torn nation,
its innocence tarnished
its peoples soul... sliced into pieces
scattered across the leftover fields, of shattered minds.

The lion roars inside his soul.
The inner Daemon of his life, has come
to view the footsteps of faith.
Am I worthy of this respect, he asks.
This fear... this burden, I now hold
within the beating, of my burning chest and soul.

Time heals all, steals all...
CHANGES ALL!

He now walks the razors edge of madness
seeking-craving-needing... vengeance.
Vengeance, on those who coveted his families blood
his sisters flesh, his inner peace.

For nothing more, then a few tic-toc's... of life.
Before the raging winter storm
wipes clean the slate of his ancestral home.
his family bones, and the remaining images
of a happy home.

The transformation begins, from boy to man.
From sane to insane.
From Hannibal
to LECTOR.

All the torn pieces of his once clean, beautiful
and full heart.
Too...

The creation, of EVIL.
The plunge into madness.
The release.
To full insanity and MADNESS!

44.

Who am I really
26 June 2018

this is not so much a poem as a philosophical thought to life.

Question:

Why is it we have an un-explainable feeling of joy, comfort and hope around a campfire or the weekend BBQ? Why is it only after the end of the camp out or BBQ, when we wash our hair in the shower, that we once again get that same feeling of joy, comfort and hope?

The answer might surprise and at the same time, mystify your very senses. Making you come to ponder and question, the very nature to the question. Who am I really?

***special note: If you're not ready, really ready for the answer... then stop. Just stop reading this now. But if you long for the explanation to an age old question, then I dare you to read on. But be warned, once read and learned, never again will you be... you. You will be the you, you've longed to be.*

Answer:

A long time ago a simple planet came into being, and after a few million years. This simple rock created life, land and the very air we breathe. This place became home to an incalculable amount of life forms. This place is our home, the rock upon witch we stand on.

Earth. Need I say more. No, yes. OK, more it is then.

In time, all things created, I.E.; land, sea, and life forms. Get destroyed. All things except the very air we breathe. Everything has been broken down and reshaped into something new, new land masses, new life forms and new bodies of water. But in all these years, never has there been any new air created. The air that was then, is the air that is now. And shall ever be, until the end of days. For this simple little planet we call earth... home.

*** *special note: Even the things and objects that can create air, is just re-releasing the air that was trapped inside of that thing or object. So once again remember. That the air we have, has always been the air, that ever has been.*

So with that fundamental knowledge under your thinking caps, ponder this. The very air we breathe is the very air, breathed by all things great and small. From the tiny microscopic creature, to the largest dinosaur ever to walk the earth. From the very dirt we live on, to the trees that filter the carbon, from the air we breathe.

The air we breathe has always been here and has always contained minuet particles, of all things that breathe in and exhale out. Why even the soil breathes, even the rocks we build upon breathe. All things on this planet, takes in air at some point, releasing it back out into and unto the world. To be partially filtered by the trees, partially... never fully filtered.

*** *special note: Trees have only a limited ability to partial filter, what ever the air is containing. Key factor here is a limited ability to filter.*

We breathe, we exhale and in doing so, we take in and release essence of our very being... our soul. So, as the trees take in the air through their leaves, they to take in the essence of everyone and everything. This is then drawn into the wood of the tree and held there until someone or some event, brings down said tree... I.E. forest fires.

We as people take this wood and use it to make our fires, to light our camp grounds... our BBQ's. And in doing so, we release the stored up essence. Essence, that has been waiting in the trees wood, waiting to be released back out unto the world. To once again ride the air currents, from where, who or what it came from.

This essence is then breathed into our lungs, soaked into our meat we smoke, then digested in our systems for nourishment. The very essence of the world as a whole, is taken into our being, giving us a connection that can't be fathomed. Not without the mind being blown away, with the fundamental understanding that we are all one.

That we have always been connected to each other and to each thing, in a way that goes beyond the physical or even the spiritual. But to the very nature of what we choose to call human beings. What we try to quantify, as life itself.

This is why you feel an undeniable connection to the campfire... to the family BBQ. This is why a smile, not only on your face but in the very core that is you, feels so right at that moment in time. And why days later, you still feel that feeling when you wash your hair and once again smell that campfire or that BBQ, riding in the air.

It's the body, the mind and the soul. Connecting to all that has been before us and reminding us that we are not alone. That we are never alone, that we are all connected and will never be forgotten. For our essence will be in the air and will live forever, until the end of days.

That is, until a giant meteor comes to wipe our very existence and even then our essence will travel along the universe's byways. Looking for another planet or planets to call home. Never can we make new air, but also never will we be forgotten, for everything and everyone rides on the currents of the air. On this planet, on that planet and even in the darkest depths of an unending universe.

So who are you-we really...? Everything and everyone, that has ever been and that will ever be.

45.

ALONE
24 July 2008

This ever pressing weight
lies, upon my heart
   in the understanding
knowledge
   that I'm completely alone.

Father... never known
ran out before
   the age of five, sets in.

Cared more
for the drink
   the drug!

Mother... abusively sick!
Never, was anything good enough.
   Complained!
Yelled!

Belt and switch
neglect an suffering
   were her true calling.

Never to have
brother, sister, aunt or uncle
   stripped away...

From any

and all family
  I could have
should have known.

46.

Loves Rejection
24 July 2008

Steps were taken
one heart reaches out
full of warmth
rainbows and sun drenched flowers
in the hopes, of a fresh start.

Two come together
each to his and her sides
with only a table between.
Orders given
to one with a smile
knowing it's their first time.

As the first words
are spoken
he can tell, in that instant
of her eye's flutter.
She's saying, you're not the one!

Realization
comes flooding in
flowers fall, heart plummets.
Each are tossed
to the ground, broken.

Broken... scattered across
the very fabric

of all.
That's unwanted
un-cherished
unloved... me!

47.

<u>Help wanted up stairs</u>
25 July 2010

Seasons come, seasons go
may the feeling of cheer
always stay with the whimsy of smile's and jeer
as only the sheer presence of him can do.

We know him as the Holy Ghost
for me he's simply dad-pop-father
unto most he gives his best
but for one who's never known.

How to express this feeling in his chest
he is absolutely-completely-undeniably the best
so I say Father my Lord, I'm ready to ascend
becoming one of the Holy Hoard.

I yearn to learn knowledge of peace and respect
then come back to the land of need, faithlessness
spreading cheer
in the form of miracles each and every year.

Oh no my son
not premature death for you... yet
for I am willing to wait
until your true time is to come, my loving son

Until then... stay there, live-laugh-love
and treat each day as your last
wait not, till your gone to spread love-cheer
for I'll always be here.

48.

Saying good night
15 may 2008

The greats all have daemons!
Chasing after their immortal soul
telling them stories of fame… of woe.

"Yes. You are woe, fame will never be yours."

Those who know a great. Count their lives as tragic
not knowing-excepting-acknowledging
who they stand behind. Act better of.

*"Try as you may, they will still be better
then you in every way."*

Why do we have to part this world
before our self worth is measured?
Found wanting, to be found exceptionable-loved
and most of all… treasured.

"Never. Never for you, my little pet."

Quiet! Say no more my little daemon
I hear you, I know my path. I've been walking it
for more lives, then I, or even you can remember.

*"Oh. I remember, my little pet. I've
been here since the beginning
and will be here, long after the end."*

So, I ask you. When does the last brick

to my road get paved? For I'm ready to sleep.
To step off this path, and take the leap to a new day.

"Yes. Take that step, its only a small step. Its only a small fall."

QUIET I SAY! For its time to shower
to say goodbye to the day and escape from you
my little daemon. In sleep-drug-drink, oh how I pray!

49.

<u>**Memories of her hug, linger on my cheek...**</u>
20 Nov 2008

Memories.
Linger, sustain
near to being strained.

In reaching for warmth.

The warmth of her cheek
caressing... my cheek
as her arms, reach around my neck.

Hands... ever so slowly
venturing down my chest
Love given, from the inner warmth
of her heart.

Memories.
Linger on a still, cold and lonely cheek
of days with movement, heat.
Perpetually glued
with my beloved, cheek to cheek.

Linger, do the memories of the past
of what once was, and never will be again.
Weary, from years of being alone!

"Long in the tooth"

As the saying goes.
Holding onto the warmth

and the cheek of my youth.

I so long-wish
You could feel the heart.
THE HEAT!

That beats in my chest, that longs...
for your sweet hands, too cares.

50.

Pool hall memories
13 May 2008

The early morning sun came into the window of Lee's small bedroom, that looked out to the parking lot of the housing complex where Lee and his family lived. The crowded complex housed multiple homes that were connected by an oval parking and a small playground behind Lee's house. Living on a military base as a kid, all of fifteen years old, was a place of loneliness and boredom, unless you were one of the beautiful people in life. Lee was a homely looking kid, very quit, shy and slightly introverted by nature. He had naturally thin soft curly light brown hair and large light brown eyes, with long eye lashes. Lee also wished to leave his little world and find freedom somewhere else, anywhere else.

The need to escape, came from a life of only being able to live in his bedroom. Except for the times when his mother let him out to do the chores and to make his own food. Ever since the age of ten, this lonely boy had been cooking his own meals. Due to the fact that his mother worked sixty hours a week and when she was off, she spent her time in her bedroom complaining of having a migraine headache. You cold actually say, that the little boy almost a man now, spent most of his entire life alone. Yes, you could say that anywhere would be a better place, then that quiet dungeon of a place he called home.

Lee was drawn from the window by the chiming of the grandfather clock down the hallway, saying it was time to come back to the real world and get the morning chores done. With one last look through the window, as the morning birds sang to the rising sun. A single tear slide down his cheek as he put his t-shirt on. He would have to get back to his dream of having friends and a loving family later. Lee could hear his mother stirring in her bedroom, getting ready for work.

"Is the coffee pot turned on," said Lee's mother as she was opening the door to her bedroom. "It better be turned on or there will be hell to pay, mister."

Lee raced to the kitchen as fast as his little legs could, to turn on the coffee pot as he yelled down the hallway to his mother that it was. Every day was the same thing, he got up at six in the morning to get the morning coffee pot turned on and to make breakfast for his unloving mother. Most days of the week, his father was already at work. Training young soldiers in the ways of the military and how to keep them alive on the battlefield.

That was when his father was even on the island, nine to ten months out of the year his father was on assignment around the world. Keeping the American people safe and warm, never knowing what has to be done to make that American dream a reality. Today was one of those rare days in the year when his father took off and stayed home, it was Lee's birthday. Lee's father Jimmy, Jim for short had promised that they were going someplace special. This special place was the reason that he had slept in and missing is usual time for getting up. He usually got up a few minutes before the old grandfather clock in the hallway range. The thought of something different from his normal routine, was the reason he stayed up far to late into the night.

Even thought Jim was Lee's step father, he had became more of a father to him, then his biological father had ever been. His own father had been a drunk and a drug user, and was known too through object's at his son when he was in a foul mood. Fortunately for Lee, he stayed for only the first four years of his young life. Divorcing his mother for a younger lady and moving to another country after his time in the army was done.

"Is the coffee done yet," said Lee's mother. "How about the eggs and toast, are they done two?"

"Almost mom. I had to open a new can and couldn't find the can opener." Said lee as he moved out of range from his mother's swing, as he walked by her getting her favorite coffee cup. A cup that could hold several servings of coffee and had a lid so she could take it to work with her without fear of it spilling in her new car. Lee tried coffee once, but after getting a head rush and then feeling weak. He gave it up for a bad idea.

Lee hoped that she wouldn't lose that infamous temper of hers this morning. It was his birthday after all and he so wanted just one of his birthdays to go well. Lee turned around with the filled cup of coffee, all the while looking for any sign that his giver of life would say two simple words. Words he couldn't remember ever hearing from his mother... happy birthday.

Lee couldn't take his eyes off of the coffee cup as he gave it to his mother, who wouldn't say happy birthday this year either. He couldn't take his off of the words on the coffee cup that said, Worlds Greatest Mother. All Lee could think of as he kept looking at those three word were, I wish.

Last years birthday was one for the record books and at the thought of that day caused a shiver to run down his spine. As he unconsciously reached up to the light scar that ran down the left side of his face. From the double-buckle belt, his mother used to punish him with when ever she thought he had done something wrong. She used to use a paddle ball to spank him with, but after the paddle had come up missing several years ago. Six years to be exact, she had turned to the dreaded double-buckle belt.

The scar went from just above his left eye, across his nose, to the lower part of his right cheek. The light scar, his mother said to the doctor that awful day one year earlier, was from her son running around in the backyard. Trying to jump over the backyard chain link fence, but in reality it was for looking her in the eyes when she told him to get outside and wash her newly bought car. It had rained hard the day before, and she didn't want to take her new car to work and have all her coworkers she her new car all dirty.

The doctor looked at him as if to say, I don't believe this for a second, but unless you give me some kind of sign, I can't help you son. Thankfully, the light scar was only temporary and the topical medicine the doctor gave his mother. Had made it disappear, nearly completely from sight, you could see a faint blemish his face if he got embarrassed or if you looked at him in just the right angle. But the memory of that day would say with him forever.

Lee knew that to say anything about what his mother did, or the extreme swings of his mother moods and temper, along with her mental and physical abuse. Which was almost daily, would only spell his death. Due to the fact that they lived in Hawaii and he was an only child and that it would be his word over hers. She was a lady who ran the finance office for the base and was well respected by everybody that worked with her. So he did the only thing available to him, he lied to the doctor and just looked down at his feet.

This was after all the mid eighties and child abuse cases were still kept secret from the public eye. Oh, most people knew that child abuse happened far more often then not, but it was better to look with blind eyes. Then to get involved in the tragedy of family affairs, that were taking place back then.

So this little boy, who wore long sleeves and long pants even in the hottest of day. Kept his fears too himself and dreamed of far away places and the day he could leave his home. But today would be different, Lee knew it would be, it had to be for his dad was home on his birthday and he said there was something special he wanted to show him.

his father was already outside as Lee came to the back door with the dog food. Lee's dog was his only real friend he had ever had, her name was Cindy, she was a beagle. She was getting older, but she could still chase a ball and give the warmest hugs and kisses with her wet tongue then any other dog could give. Kisses that were the only ones he had ever had, she was his world and she was getting older. He feared for the day when he would have to say goodbye to her, because then he would truly be all alone in this cruel world he was born into.

As Lee opened the back door, Cindy came running in from the backyard where she was watching Lee's dad working on a part of the fence that needed mending. It was coming loose at the bottom and Cindy had gotten out the other day, he could still feel the welts on his backside, where his mother had whipped him with that double-buckle belt.

Cindy ran up to him trying to jump into his out stretched arm, but instead just waited for him to lean down and decided that several wet kisses would have to do instead. Lee watched her eat for a minute or two, then went outside to start picking up the dog poop and to start raking the leaves, it was the end of September and the leaves were a constant bother for him. The leaves collected at the bottom of the fence and even though Cindy was getting older, she could still poop like a puppy with a full belly of yummy dog food.

But today was different, there wasn't any leaves to be raked up and his father had already collected up all the dog poop. A small amount of fear crawled up Lee's spine as he thought to himself "I hope they aren't sending me to military school, my grades weren't that bad last year."

"Well, I see you finally decided to join the land of the living," said Lee's dad as he started to laugh out loud. It was a warm and deep laugh, that always made him feel safe, even though he couldn't tell his dad why.

"Thats from the movie we watched last night," said Lee thinking of the movie they had watched last night. Whenever his dad was home for more then a few days at a time. Especially Sunday nights, the two of them would stay up and watch the first of the late, late show movies. It wasn't really that late, it was only nine-o-clock but it felt late to him. Since he had to be in his room all the time when his dad was away, and his mother didn't want him outside of his bedroom, at any time of the day or night. Along with him having to be in bed asleep by eight-o-clock.

"Yep, thats right I should have known I couldn't put one past on you," said Lee's dad. "What with you knowing every horror movie ever made." Lee didn't actually know every horror movie ever made, but he did remember all the movies he had ever seen with his dad. His dad had a thing for horror movies and being this close to Halloween. His dad made sure that when he was home, Lee and him would watch the latest scary movie they had at blockbusters.

Lee hated to change the subject, because he lived for these simple little moments with his stepfather. A man who had taken the place of his real father. A father who beat him with anything that came into his grungy little hands, for no reason at all. He was a drunk, a drug user, along with being a terrible husband and an all around angry human being.

His stepfather had come into his life when he was four years old, and had officially adopted him when he was five, giving Lee his last name instead of his birth fathers last name. In the ten years that his stepfather had come into his life, he had tried his best to teach his values unto his adopted son, values that his father governed his life with. One of honor, respect for all things, pride in what you do and taking full blame for what you have done wrong.

But unfortunately, the only thing he unknowingly did was to always remind Lee, that he needed to give a hundred percent in what ever he did. His father would continually say "Instead of always doing things half ass, do them right the first time." Even though Lee did his very best each and ever day, for fear of his mother beating him when his dad was away. Even though his dad would continue to tell him to stop doing things half ass, Lee would let it slide. Because his stepfather in all ten years, had never raised a single finger to him in anger.

"So dad, what is this surprise you were telling me about last night," said Lee as he looked up to his father, who stood six foot three and him barely standing four foot eleven.

"Well now, lets see why don't you go to the front of the house and get my jacket off the hook." Said Lee's dad, with a great big smile on his chiseled face. "Then meet me out by the truck and I'll take you to the surprise I was telling you about last night."

At hearing this Lee ran to the back door where Cindy was just finishing her morning breakfast. He dropped down for a split second to give his girl a warm hug and a big kiss on her cold wet nose. Cindy wagged her short tail, giving a wet lick back, then went to the water bowl to wash down the last reminisces of the dog food left in her cheeks.

Lee opened the back door, all the while spitting out the taste of dog food onto his long sleeve shirt from the wet kiss Cindy had given him. By the time Lee had gotten to the front door, his dad had already made his way around the house and was waiting by the front door. Lee saw his dad and gave him his leather coat and then they both made their way with his dads black ford two door step side truck. His fathers pride and joy.

Lee never noticed the small bead of sweat, that was forming at the edge of his dad's hairline. From jumping over the backyard fence and sprinting all the way around the house to beat his son to the front door. Jim was looking forward to this day with his son, even more then son was. It was one of Jim's favorite things to do with his father when he was a kid and now it was time that he introduced his son to one of his favorite games to play.

They both jumped into the truck with smiles on their faces and as the engine fired up and the eight track player turned on, his dad hit play. Starting his dads favorite music group, Journey. They both joined in as the song started to blast of the two six by six speakers, his father had installed the last time he was home. Speakers that hung precariously in the upper rear corners of the single bench seated truck cab.

As the music played and they truck made its way to the secret destination, they sang with the tape and had large and genuine smiles on their faces. All the while, Lee looked out the window enjoying the five mile trip to the backside of the Army base. Where the old warehouses resided, most of them nearly one hundred years old, and sat empty and alone. But a few of them were being converted to stores and places of entertainment, like the one Lee and his dad were pulling up to.

Lee looked out the front window at the red bricked building with the very large sign saying, 'Now open, come one come all to Larry's Pool Hall.'

Larry's Pool Hall, was newly opened only one month ago. Lee's dad had found out about it from some of his buddies in his unit, they said it was a family oriented pool hall. Where anyone from the base could go and learn to play billiards for free. They even held tournaments for kids and teenagers, and even team competitions for the adults and for two family members to compete as well.

Jim looked at his son's face as he turned off the trucks engine. The smile and wonderment in his boys big brown eyes were all the thanks you could ever wish for. These were the moments Jim lived for, and wished he could have more of, but his duty to his country and his family had to come first. He was an officer in the United States of America, and he had made a promise to defend his country even though it took him away from his family that he cherished most in this world.

"Lets go tiger," said Jim as he looked again at his son. "Lets see if you can take your old dad in a game or two of pool."

"But I don't know how to play pool dad." Said Lee, as a small worried look started to take over the large smile on his sons face.

"Don't worry son, I'll teach you," said Jim. "I used to shoot pool with your grandfather when I was a kid, and I still remember all that he taught me back then."

The double doors were already opened and the sounds of cracking and racking balls, could be heard just outside by Lee and his dad. Even though it was only eight in the morning, several of the tables were already taken. But Lee could see one in the far right corner that was still unoccupied.

"Dad, there's a table over there in the corner still open," said Lee. "Can we get that one?" Lee jumped up and down, hardly able to contain his excitement bottled up inside his small body.

"We have to check in with the gentlemen at the desk first before we can get a table," said Jim, as a small smile came to his face and a smaller laugh crept out the side of his mouth. "That one might already be spoken for."

Lee's dad had already called down to the pool hall yesterday, to reserve a table in the corner, so he and his son could have one ready for them when they arrived. Lee took the pool stick and raced over to the corner table he had seen when they walked in, he could see that there was something on the green felt.

As he came closer he could see a long box with a small bow attached to it sitting on the green felt that covered the beautiful wooden pool table, along with a box of Dunkin Doughnuts next to it with a card saying happy birthday to the best boy in the world, love dad. He stopped at the side of the pool table afraid to touch the green felt, for fear that this was one of his many dreams and by touching the table it would come to an abrupt end.

End it didn't, it was just the beginning of something wonderful for Lee and his dad and it would be one of the best days, in Lee's life and it would be one of the best days in his fathers life as well. Lee was brought out of his short daydream, to his dad racking the balls on the table and calling his name.

"Come over here tiger, let me show you how to rack the balls," said Jim. "So what do you think of your very own pool stick. Why you haven't even taken off the bow yet. Now how are you going to play if it's still in its case." A small tear ran down his cheek as he saw the pride on his little mans face, as he reached out for the blue felt case and opened the wooden box, containing the newly bought two hundred dollar pool stick.

They spent the first hour running through a few different types of shots and two different types of games, one being eight ball and the other being nine ball. After the second game of nine ball, Lee started to get hot and decided to take off his jacket. Which was really a long sleeve shirt made of flannel, one of his favorites. It was a red and black flannel shirt that his dad had given him several years ago. Lee couldn't wear regular jacket due to his naturally elevated body temperature.

In the early days of fall, when the winds of the island would start to blow cold air, Lee could be seen wearing his father's long sleeve flannel shirt every day. Whether it was inside or out. As he started to take off the flannel shirt, his father caught a glimpse of a large black and blue mark on his son's left arm.

"What is that on your arm?" asked Jim as he was raking up the balls for the next game.

Lee looked down at his arm, then up again at this dad with a worried look on his face. He knew he had to come up with something fast, so as not to ruin the day. "Nothing dad, its just a bruise from gym class last Friday. Said lee. "We were playing dodge ball and I took a ball to the chest and then tripped over another ball and went town on my left side."

"Well is you arm OK,"said Jim. "Do we need to have the doctor look at it? It could be broken."

Lee pulled up the flannel shirt and waved his arm showing his dad that everything was OK, then quickly grabbed his pool stick, getting ready to break the balls as his dad had shown him earlier.

Jim looked at his son for a second or two, before the thought he was thinking was pulled out of his head, as a white ball came flying by. A ball which nearly took off his head. Jim's took a few seconds to tell the guys on the next table to be a little more careful with their breaks and made his way back to his own pool table. The question of was his son telling the truth about the bruise was forgotten, when he saw his son give all the gusto he had to breaking the racked balls.

"What an excellent break that was tiger," said Jim. "I couldn't have done any better myself. Now thats how you open up the table and it looks like you dropped a ball of each type.

Which one do you want to go for, strips or solids?" All thoughts of the bruise was gone.

Lee took a quick look at the table, as his dad told him to do and saw that the stripes were the better play. "I'll take stripes dad." And with the next stroke of the pool stick, he made a total mess of his shot, sending ball of both types all over the table. Lee had done this on purpose, so his dad would think that he had already forgotten how to set up a shot.

Lee wanted his dad's thoughts off his bruise, the one his mother gave him just two days ago, for accidentally tipping over his mothers flower vase and sending the glass rocks and fake flowers all over the wooden floor in the living room. Thankfully his dad couldn't see the very large bruise to his back and the smaller bruises to the back of his upper legs, from that dreaded double-buckle belt. If he had, then they would of left the pool hall and his dad would of taken him to the doctors right away. Then he would of went home to confront his wife to why there were so many bruises on his sons body.

But thankfully his dad just laughed at the total mess of a shot and said don't worry about it son, I used to make all kinds of mistakes when I first started to learn how to play pool. As the day went on, people would come and go, but he table in the far right corner never changed and the two people there played for the rest of the day. With many laughter and banters coming from this small corner of the world.

Both of them held onto this day for as long as they could, holding on to it with hungered grip. For each knew that when the day came to an end, each of them would have to go back to the real world and the problems that came along with them. Lee with the feeling of being alone in the world and Jim with the responsibilities of being and officer in the United States Army.

For Lee's dad, it was the ever calling arm of the Army and

the missions he was called to do for President and Country. For Lee it would be two more years of neglect, abuse and the lonely world of his dreams. Still there were to be moments like these, even though they would be few and far in between in the next two years. When Lee and his father would come to the pool hall, trying to recapture that first moment even if its for only a day or two.

But for that little boy, wishing for manhood to come all the sooner, that first day at the pool hall would be held in his memories. And drawn upon when the darker days would come, when he pondered on taking his own life.

Lee held these dreams and many more in his head and heart though the last two years of his childhood. They would become his world when lonely days of pain would enter his small room. He would hold onto them when his mothers drunken rage would show and she would blame him, that he was the reason for her pitiful life. That he was the cause of her never graduating high school due to her getting pregnant at sixteen. And it was his fault that she could make something more of herself. And he would hold onto those dreams when she would lash out with fist and with the double-buckled belt

This little boy would keep all he felt inside, until graduation day. When he would join the military and create his own life, one that would have its own sadness and pain. But the dreams of the past would never leave and in the future they would start to call out to be seen and heard.

This little boy who wanted to escape his house of hell. Would start to learn how to write and the tears of a lonely past, would start to wash away in the form of poetry and hopefully a story someday.

The End.

51.

Old lady, old bench and a mouse
05 Jan 2009

Question for you:

What constitutes a family, what makes it real? Is it the interactions of one to the other or just the love thats required to be there, due to bloodline or marriage? Or could it be something as simple as the freely given time and emotional support of one creature to another? In their happy days, sad days and in their time of dire need. By just being there by their side, through the good, the bad, the tough and the sad times in their lives. Would this not be called family too... if there was no blood ties between the two of you?

So I send out this question. To you the reader. As you view a simple old lady on a bench. It is said, you never know someone until you walk a mile in their shoes. Trod the path their foot steps have taken them on. So I give this to you. A simple day at the park, any park in any city, state or even country. Where you see an old lady sitting on an old park bench. Do you look her way, or just pass her by? Consumed with the closed mindedness of your world, never giving first thought to those around you. Because they may actually need you, may actually matter.

So ponder and think, as you read. For if this was someone else passing by that old lady, and stopped to say hello. To find out who she is, and if they needed help. She could very well be related to him or her, me or even you. For do we really know all of our friends, relatives and loved ones by sight alone... well do we?

Part One:

She watches the young people go by, busily about their daily lives. Sadden for their lose, their emptiness, their greed. She worries. For the humanity of their souls, are in question. For their love of all things materialistic has taken over, replacing their soul of compassion in each other, hope in each other and faith of each other. For the love of all things created by hand, instead of cherishing the humanly bond of each other instead.

All of these things and so many more of forgotten emotions, now reside in the growing tinder box, that used to be their faith. Faith in each other and in an absent landlord, who's been neglecting his children. For far to long. Their tender box lies only inch's away, from the eternal pit of Hell itself. Teetering on the edge of oblivion.

Needing only one more emotion, not given out freely, but tossed aside willingly.

Thrown inside their tinderbox of fate. This and so many other things, does this little old lady, on a simple old park bench see, but hopes will never come to pass. As all the lost souls pass her bye. Never giving a second thought to her life, her wellbeing and her safety.

This little old lady in her golden years of life, sits on an aging park bench, nearly as old as she. Made by her deceased lover, some sixty years or so ago. A tattered old thing, that still shows some of its grander and elegance, from a time long ago, if only you looked onto it in the right light.

The young walk by, hugging and kissing on each other for the pleasure of the minute, the moment. No longer for the everlasting time thats given to us all. Whether it be ten, twenty or even fifty years of a faithful marriage. No, they love only for the split second they can achieve the other they greed for, desire for in that moment in time.

When someone actually takes the time to look upon this little old lady, sitting on the tired old wooden bench. They cringe, at the sight of a sitting charcoal of a human being looking back at them. Her in her tattered old cloths and her multiple hand bags. Which hold all her earthly belongings by her side, in an old rusty shopping cart. They never really see the pain in her eyes, or the welcoming smile upon her seared, scared and tortured face.

They don't see the bend in her back, from years work on the rack of life. Trying to make a meager wage in the days of... *"you stay home and make the baby, take car of the babe, feed the baby, and me! Every day, for your not meant to make the pay and be with him."*

It was strange, she could still remember her father yelling those same words to her as she took her newly born daughter of only three weeks, and all her belongings she owned out into the as of yet unknown and scary world. All of it carried in one simple little suitcase, in her left had as she held her dear little baby girl in her right hand. She was only sixteen years old. But who was... him? That strangers face she always saw as she fell asleep. It was the only memory that came to her in the dead of night, lying in her simple cardboard box. A place she's called home for many a year now.

Part Two

She sat there on her bench, rubbing a tear away from her left eye, as she ate the sandwich she found in the trash can behind the deli, just around the corner of her home in the local park. The mayonnaise is fouled more then a week now, maybe even two from the how deep it was laying in the trash can. She had seen just the corner of it poking out as she was walking bye on her way back to the park and her bench she called home. She takes another bite musing to herself, ignoring the taste as she ponders what her name is, a name long forgotten to time along with her memories of the past.

Home, it sounded weird that someone would call such a place as Leper's Field a home, but the indigent go to where they are wanted, or pushed as her case was. Pushed away by the pain in a young daughters eyes, at the sight of her mother she no longer knows. Pushed away by the pain, anger, torment and foul language thats taken hold of her once proud, beautiful and powerful mind. A mind now tormented, ravaged and traumatized by the tumors running ramped in her tired old brain.

The abandoned inner city block of Twenty Third Street and Johnson, also known as Leper's Field. It's called this due to the continuous amount of people contracting deadly diseases. Diseases that make the flesh change color even fall off of their very own bodies. These people who call it home, getting sick from the uncleanliness of the place. They get sick from eating all the rotten food from the local low end restaurants trash cans out back in the dark and dangerous alleyways. Even from the local populace who have passed away, by those who walk on the other side of sanity. Yes, Lepers Field is home to the unwanted citizens of the tired old and battered city.

Leper's Field is in the center of the city, made up of five square blocks of torn down buildings, of what once old wall street. And a once great church of Christ, that has holes in the roof and the rear wall lying in the once prized and beautiful cemetery from years ago. A church that still houses one old priest, the only one who still cares for the lost, confused and thrown away people of Leper's Field.

Part Three

Her smile was the only thing of two on her damaged face that still held its once heavenly beauty, the other being her cobalt blue eye's. Eye's that had the ability to make even the vilest of people, wishing to earn her honor, love and friendship. She would only look back at the one's brave enough to look her way, for her tongue was taken from her twenty years ago, when she first came to Leper's Field.

Even those from Leper's Field wouldn't tolerate her foul mouth, but they had a solution. A simple answer with a permanent solution, if she didn't have a tongue then she couldn't say those foul words she has become famous for. It was known by those who called Leper's Field home, to stay away from the one with the cobalt eyes. Because her nasty and foul mouth could bring even the hardened tramp of Leper's Field to their knee crying from pain and shame. Even though they took her tongue she still stayed.

Even when the local business owners stepped in with the intention to burn the plague of the bums out of Leper's Field with a cleansing fire. And even after they took her beauty away in a fire that was meant too cleanse the inner blocks and park of Leper's Field. She still stayed at her wooden bench. And for twenty years she's called this place of darkness and sadness... home.

These days only the squirrels and the occasional mouse that came her way, could hear the mumblings of her gurgling, as she told stories of yesterdays while she feed them with her moldy bread on her lover's wooden bench. Stories that came to her destroyed mind as she watched the squirrels play in the grand old oak tree, that stood not more then five feet behind and to the right of the tired old wooden bench she was sitting on.

Many a day she survived on nothing but the nuts that fell out of the old oak tree, the same tree that the squirrels she now fed. She knew not if they fed her, or if it was by accident that the nuts collected by these little four legged angels from heaven. That just happened to fall out of their mouth's, or did it happen on purpose? This happened when she was sitting on her bench and only when she was sitting on her wooden bench. And when she wasn't at her lovers wooden bench she would find nuts lying next to the front right metal leg of her lovers wooden bench.

Today was one of those days when her little buddy, Missy mouse came to visit. She always loved it when her little mouse friend came by, she always brought something delicious to eat with her. A small bit of cheese or even a piece of freshly cooked meat. They would both share the delicious morsel, a morsel that anybody else would become sick at the very thought, of taking food from a dirty little mouse. One that probably had rabies, or something even worse, like Ebola.

As the young people strolled by her bench they scoffed, even shrieked at seeing her eating with a foul dirty rodent. Some even threw things at her as they made fun of the way she looked and the state she was in, never once taking the time to really look at her. Never once does the emotions of anger, hatred or revenge venture into her loving heart. She just wept small tears every now and then as they made fun of her. Even after all of this mistreatment of her way of life, she still prayed to God to forgive them and all the things they did to her.

It wasn't always like this, there were days when she was totally alone. Even on the days when the sun was out, birds sang to her while she watched her little friends playing in her favorite oak tree, planted by her long lost lover. On these days she felt like the only person left in the world, but her favorite days were when the park was full of people.

Even though the park was in the worst area of the old town, it was still one of the most beautiful places to visit. And those who were brave to enter Leper's Field and walk the stone pathways of Leper's Field Park were rewarded with views of the once great past of the tired old city with the incredible stone statues and the famous trees and plants from all over the world. Even if the visitors didn't want her presence messing up their idea of the perfect day.

Today wasn't one of those days. Missy mouse sat at the the old ladies side while she ate some of the sausage this remarkable little mouse had found for her. If anyone actually took the time to watch this little mouses comings and goings, they would see something amazing. They would see a strange almost loving relationship between the small mouse and the aging lady who called this ordinary wooden bench, by any other persons eyes, home.

At least in the day time hours, before the cops would push her, nearly forcing her out of the park, before the shadows of the chilly night would take control. If these people looked a little harder they would see and almost get the feeling the little mouse knew her. And if they stayed to look even closer, they would see a small little paw that would at times reach out to an old wrinkled hand.

Patting it lovingly.

Part Four

All day long she would stay on her bench, sitting at times, laying at other times looking up at the clouds as they rolled on by, making those funny shapes that brought a smile to her once lovely sad and scared face. Other times she would rub her aged hands over the wood, knowing that her lover had once did the same thing as he was making it for her.

A flash of a memory sped through her mind, bits and pieces of her lover saying that he found this old piece of wood on one of his archaeological trips. He was always going on these digs, looking for things of import to the history of Jesus Christ when he was alive. He was a man of the cloth, but lived among the people of the here and now. Choosing to dig up the past, instead of talking about the good book alone.

He was also and avid carpenter, wanting to be more like the son of God. He loved to make rocking chairs, but the local chapter wanted him to make some bench's. Bench's to be given to the local park with a golden plate on the backrest, with a quote from different parts of the bible. Giving inspiration to all who might sit on it, and chose to read what was written, hopefully choosing to be saved by the Lord or God.

After she ate her sausage, giving half of it to Missy mouse, she stretched out lying down for a mid-days nap with Missy mouse, who was sitting by her head. Softly stroking her once golden hair with the little paw of a friend, or maybe it was a lover...? There they both watched the clouds go by, blanking out the world for a little while. Letting the passer-byers go about their own business and their own lives.

In these moments of restfulness and peace, she felt as if her head was laying on the lap of her long dead lover. Peace would come to her in these moments when her little friend could spend time with her. She knew not were her little friend went or why her little mouse friend spent so much time away and where a little mouse could want to go. She just excepted the time given to her, with a deep and warming smile to her face as she slipped into a wonderful dreamy sleep. Remembering her lover's hands working on this very bench she slept on at this very moment.

As she slipped further into a deep peaceful and relaxing sleep, the little mouse stroked her hair one more time, before taking off. To once again, continuing the search, looking for... her. The little mouse climbed down the bench, running across the dirt and stone pathway. Sliding in-between the people walking by, looking back only once to the other side of the pathway, making sure she was still asleep and safe.

The little mouse came to the edge of the five mile park, that weaved its way around the inner cities by-ways of the once grand, popular and populated metropolitan city. The hub of a young but growing nation, now just an old and tattered shell aged and warn just like the sleeping old lady lying on her bench. Her once and glorious days, now long gone too the wayside of more popular, visually young cities. Cities that have grown up on the edge of the nation, taking in the sea and surf giving the young an endless amount of things to do.

As if by design the little mouse went this way and that, the mental map in its head keeping everything its sees and everywhere the little mouse has been. Keeping it at the ready, so as not to go over the same thing and the same place twice. For a city is a very large place for one little mouse to search, especially if its searching for someone who too is searching. Searching for the mother she has wronged, lost some twenty odd years ago now.

Every day this strange little mouse searches the streets of this tired old city, looking for a daughter a mother no longer remembers. And every day this little mouse comes back to the bench just in time to watch the little old lady wake up. The mouse watches her sit up turning around reaching out to rub the small piece of wood in the middle of the golden plate. Then watching her collect her things, all the while looking around for her little friend, saddened at her little friends absence. She stands and begins the trip back home to Leper's Field, going back to her card board box that she calls home. Too her precious belongings, one's that she no longer remembers, or even knows why she continues to keep.

Part Five

This strange and mysterious mouse walks behind the

little old lady, as she pushes her shopping cart of trinkets, collected too try and sell at the corner of Johnson and Eight, known as Gobbs End. A place were you could buy and sell just about anything legal or not legal. She comes to the trash filled curb section of Gobbs End where she usually tries to sell her collected odds and ends, too anyone who would be willing to buy from her, but nobody was there. Autumn was quickly changing to the beginning of winter and the weather was coming on hard and fast.

The colder days of September, was keeping the sane people inside at this time of the day, even the slightly insane people didn't want to temp fate. What with the dark storm clouds barreling its way into the city from the north. Whispering a harsh and deadly winter yet to come, many would not see the new year and the warm days of spring to come.

A storm sure to take more then a few lives of the indignant and sick living in Leper's Field. The old lady choosing to make her way back home, deciding not to wait and see if anyone would come out to Gobbs End to buy her odds and ends. Came to a small discarded double sided refrigerated shipping box made of double walled corrugated card board, her home. She smiled seeing her little dilapidated home and set her shopping cart to the side, got down on her scared and arthritic knees and crawled inside. It was an unwritten rule that if anything was left outside beside shopping carts it was free game to whoever came upon it, but nobody wanted to take anything form the crazy old lady who lived behind that rusted old door.

She looked inside once, then turned around to the opening, then closed the make shift door made from a rusted tailgate off an old nineteen sixty four Chevy truck. She used to use a broken piece of glass for her door, but it kept on cutting her hands when she tried to move it one way or the other. Until one day she came too her home and found her current door in its place instead of the broken glass. Not just in place but hinged to the side, it even had small metal wheels attached to the bottom outer corner, so it could be rolled back and forth for easer movement.

She never knew who had made the door, but she had a feeling deep inside that it was the little old man at the end of the alley who every now and then looked in on her. Even leaving food with only a single knock on the metal Chevy door, letting her know that something was outside for her.

The next day was an exception, she had gotten up and walked past the little old mans home made of discarded doors and tin roofing on her way to the park. The door was opened, she looked inside and saw someone else lying inside. She knew then and there that the little old man who had been so kind to her, if it was he that left all the little scrapes of food had passed away sometime in the night. It was the way of things, when someone died another person would come and claim what ever was there, even the very clothes and home they lived in.

The next night's cold northern wind came down even harder, it came down with the teeth of the wolf, as the saying goes and it came to bit. It came to sink and tear its hungry fangs into anyone unlucky enough to fall asleep outside. Death road on the wind and the little mouse knew, it was only a matter of time before it would come calling. Calling for the little old lady, the mouse visited every day, the mouse knew he had very little time left. He just had to get the young girl and the little old lady he loved together, before both of their times were up.

With a renewed vigor in his little heart, the little mouse went out into the bitterly cold norther wind, searching once again for her. Its ears were numb from the effort and energy it spent that night, but his search was rewarded, he had found her. She was going into an upscale home on the outer edge of the northern side of town. The little mouse ran as hard as his little legs would carry him, but he was unable to get to the front door in time to get inside before the door closed right in front of his frozen whiskered little runny nose.

The little mouse curled up as best as he could in an old rusty tin can just inside the sewer grate next to the door the young lady had gone into, trying its best to keep warm. Waiting for the young lady to come out again, wanting to make sure it was her before it went for the crumpled old letter, now yellowed with age and years of neglect.

The mouse was stirred to wakefulness by the opening of the front door as the young and beautiful lady came out the front door, just before the rising of the morning sun. He looked at her under the front porch light, she had the same eyes, nose even the small triangular chin that was a calling mark of the ladies in her family. Yes, it was her, he just knew it. The strange little mouse took off immediately, she had to know, they had to know before it was too late…

Part Six

Off he scampered in the early rising sun light, straight as an arrow to the home of the little old lady. He knew that she would be rising soon, making her way to the bench, stopping only here and there to look into the trash cans and the rarely used alleyways looking for trinkets to sell at Gobbs End. The little mouse looked up only once at the rising sun and it looked to be a beautifully sunny day.

The little mouse didn't take the time to wait at the home of the young lady, he didn't see what happened next. So the little mouse didn't see the lady walk back inside, coming out with a twelve old girl and get inside their SUV. Driving out of the neighborhood heading to the freeway ramp, pointing west.

Speeding like gossamer, the SUV races to its destination, as too does this strange little mouse. One's destination is a weekend at Disneyland and the other's destination is to ketch up with the little old lady, before she arrives at the bench. Its own destination just as important. Even more with the weather speeding on the wings of hell itself, even though the sun shined bright as the little mouse came to the edge of Leper's Field. So to did the bit in the wind as if the wolves, were not wolves at all, but the hounds of hell pushing the cold of the north down upon Leper's Field and the on this fallen city of yesteryears.

The little mouse rushed over what was left of the green grass, passing patch's of brown here and there from dogs reliving themselves, he sped between the people as they played Frisbee, flying kits and playing football. Risking his very own life in the process of trying to get back in time to see her, to sit with her knowing that she would be well into her morning reading. Reading what ever she could find on her way to the park and her lovers wooden bench. He knew if she found a book or magazine she would be reading it to the squirrels she loved so much.

He came upon her lying not sitting as was her usual thing to be doing at this time of the day. She was curled up into a ball, with one hand griping tightly to the slime crusted and moldy leather trench coat, all the while coughing violently. As her other hand trembled as it stroked the small piece of wood, that was in the middle of the golden plate surrounded by strange markings.

The little mouse crawled up her dangling pants leg, traveled over her curved back too the thin brittle graying hair and curled up by her cheek. Reaching out with its little paw, trying to give what little warmth it had to give to the lady it loved so very much. He squeaked into her right ear as she laid there, attempting to hold onto what ever warmth she could, praying to God she would see another one of his glorious shinny days.

God has a strange way of answering his lost children. Its not always in the form or in the thing we want, and it may not even be known to us, that he is lessoning and that he has answered our prayers. Sometimes it came through a burning bush, other times its something smaller less noticeable... like a strange little mouse and a bench.

The little mouse told her of its day. Of how it followed her home last night like he usually did and how he went out into the bitter wind all night looking for the one she needed so much. And how this amazing little mouse, had finally found her in this modest little home in a very nice neighborhood. He told her how he had raced back to her home in the early morning hours, to get a very old and special letter.

A letter that had been written so many years ago, some twenty or so years now. And how he went back to the home of the younger lady. Slipped the yellowing and somewhat stained letter under the front door, then how he ran all the way back to her. To let her know that she had been found and it should be any time now, that the younger lady will show up taking her to her home. A real home where she will be loved, be warm and wanted for the rest of her days.

But the younger lady didn't come. And the end of autumn days, turned into one of the deadliest winter anyone could remember in the last hundred years. More people would die this winter, then all of the last one hundred years joined together. Thats what the little old lady had heard from several people standing outside of an electronics store.

Several days after the day the little mouse had found the young lady he was looking for, she kept on hearing this on her way back to her bench in the park. Her fever getting worse with every painful step she took, wanting nothing more then to be warm and to see her little friend Missy mouse.

Part Seven

The young lady didn't even know there was a letter, for when they came home that Sunday there was no letter at the base of the front door. It had been blown under the door side table out of sight out of mind. It took almost two months before the little girl found the letter, after she came inside from playing in the gathering snow at the back of the house.

It was only due to her falling down as she crossed the thresh hold of the front door seal that she saw it at all. If it wasn't for that simple miss step then the letter might of never been found, and if it hadn't been found at that moment in time it may have been to late. It may still be too late.

The little mouse told the old day of how it went every night to the young ladies home and waited outside till the morning. And he told her of how he found out that the lady had a beautiful daughter, but every morning was the same thing they never saw the little mouse. They would come outside and stand at the front door of there cute Spanish style two story house for a little while, while both of them waited for the school bus to arrive.

Then he told her of the great oak tree in the front yard that the mother would stand under, while she waited for the young girl to walk to the bus and the bus to leave for another day of school. Then the mother would get into her large SUV and make her way to the small art studio she owned. Where she would paint and sculpt all day long until it was time to come back home. To once again stand under the great oak tree, once again waiting for her little angle to step off the bus and brighten her long and tiring day up.

Then the mouse told her of how he followed her every day, and how he would follow her as far as he could until she went out of his sight. Then the next day he would stand at that exact location he lost her, and then take off when she passed him. To once again chase after her, until once again the large SUV left his sight. He told her it had taken a week for him to finally reach the location to here she went every morning after her daughter got onto the bus.

After nearly two months of dedicated vigil of watching her home in the mornings, the little mouse gave up, not because he didn't have faith. No, it was due to his lady love the one who fed and told stories to him, was becoming sick… no, she was already sick. She was getting sicker by the day. Something had to change or the little mouse just knew it would be to late for the old lady, and for him. But for the first time in this strange little brown mouse life, with the white spot in the center of his cute little forehead. He didn't know what to do, but he could feel the fear creep into his even smaller little mouse's heart.

It was just after the new year, a day or so, if the mouse was correct with its calculations and the early morning sun was about to rise up for a new day. He knew that this was her favorite time of the day, she always got up to see the mornings sunrise. She always told the little mouse that the new rays of the sunshine, was God opening his eye's and how he looked down upon hi creations. Saying, I haven't forgotten you my children, my love, my hope.

This day it was different, the little mouse sat outside waiting for her, but she just kept on lying on the lice infested mattress that she called a bed. The little mouse went back inside to see if everything was OK, but found her still lying down fast asleep. With sweat running down her forehead, and her skin burning as if the very flames of hell, were trying to come through and burn down her lice infested home and her beautiful soul.

The little mouse ran its paw across her face, she opened her eye's just a little and knew she had missed the morning sunrise for the first time that she could remember. With a monumental amount of effort she raised her tired old body, and started to make her way to her bench. The little mouse held onto her neck as she pushed her rusted cart down the trash filled side walk of leper's Field, past Gobbs End and over the brown grass of the old park. Making her way back to her bench, her hope... and her lover's embrace.

The little old lady was lying on the bench, absently stroking the small piece of wood once again the center of the golden plate. Her eyes closed to the world, trying to warm herself with the blanket the little mouse had found for her. Where with the help of some crafty little squirrels, they brought it to her, just a few minutes ago.

She chewed on another nut that happened to be left in the center of the for mentioned, somewhat stolen blanket from that nice couple, who left it there when they got up to leave. She also found a small pile of nuts at the front corner of the bench, she reached out her tired, red and swollen hand to pick another one up. Placing it into her mouth as she tried to curl up even smaller so the little blanket would cover her whole sore ridden body at one time.

The little mouse made its way to her neck once again and curled up there stroking her ear, as she reached out for another nut with one hand and the other one lovingly rubbing the small piece of wood in the golden plate. All the while listening to the wind as it blew its song of death, to anyone crazy enough to be outside on a day like this. Until the wind was blocked by something or someone, she turned her head towards the dirt pathway, towards that something or someone. And saw a small but beautiful little girl standing not more then a foot from her scared and scary face. Smiling! Smiling the smile of innocence and love.

She had long lost the ability to be surprised, twenty years or so of living in Leper's Field and sitting on her bench, lessoning to the passer-biers saying and sailing all manner of words and objects. One loses some abilities with a life like hers, like being surprised. So she just laid there looking at this cute little girl with the cobalt eyes, as the little girl looked back at the old lady on the bench with a strange little mouse curled up at her neck.

Just as the little girl was going to open her mouth to say hello. The old lady on the bench began a cough that would take several minutes to finish. The little girl and her mother looked down upon this sad, thrown away and near to death lady, and both started to cry.

It was those tears that stopped the coughing, and had another effect on the tired old lady on the warn out bench. She was shocked and as she sat up, she had a strange feeling in the pit of her mostly empty stomach. She wasn't sure… but, no it couldn't be… yes it was, she was surprised. Surprised by the strangers tears, tears for her not because of her.

As the little lady sat up she was careful of Missy mouse still sitting on her neck, now sitting on her shoulder and looking up at her. Then to the little girl and then lastly to the mother at her side, as they waited for her to say something, anything. Not understanding why she didn't say a world, any word.

It took more then five minutes for this little old lady on the wooden bench to figure out what she wanted to say, she couldn't even remember when was the last time anyone had spoken to her. She hadn't said anything to anyone other then the gurgling she made, when she told her stories to Missy mouse. And the little squirrels from the old tree her late husband had planted, to many years for her to remember now.

Then as if a bolt of lightning had shot from Odin's godly hand, she did something that shocked all three. She opened her mouth, showing them that she had no tongue to speak with, and tears came out from her beautiful cobalt blue eyes.

Part Eight

Mother and daughter raised their hands to their face, not

in terror and not in fear, but in pain. Pain at the understanding that she couldn't say hello, say goodbye. She couldn't say anything and it was in that knowledge and understanding that made those tears gush out of their eyes sliding down their soft non-scared cheeks and fall the the ground in front of the little old lady sitting on the worn out wooden bench.

The mother of the little girl feared as her heart leaped into her throat, then plummeted down into the depths of worry and despair, now fear crept into her mind. Not at the tragedy of what happened to this little old ladies mouth, but that she may not, will not come home with them. Or even remember her... her daughter.

The old lady tried to mumble the words "may I help you, are you lost?" Instead it came out in a sickly gurgle, that no one in their right mind would ever be able to understand in a million years. But she did, she didn't understand how but she understood exactly what her mother had said, so did her daughter. She wiped a fresh tear that was getting ready to fall from her eye "no mother I am not lost, its me your daughter and this beautiful little angel is Isabella."

The little old lady just sat there for a moment or two as the words bounced around in her scrambled tired old mind. Then as if the vale had been lifted, a giant smile came to her scared face, as the realization of what the young lady said made complete since to her. She once again mumbled incoherent words to all of them, but saw that the little girl was no longer paying attention, she was sitting on the bench next to her grandmother. While the little strange mouse was sitting in her hands, patting her little hand ever so lovingly.

"I... I... I remember you," said the old lady, "but who is this beautiful little angel sitting next to me holding Missy mouse?" Had anyone else been outside on a bitter cold day as this, they would of only heard gurgling from the old lady. That is if they even took the time to look their way at her, and the two nice people taking an interest in her.

"Why mother she is your granddaughter Isabella," said Sofia as she kneeled down next to her daughter. As she reached out to her grandmother for the first time, taking her hard, cold, reddened and cracked right hand in her tinny warm one. Missy mouse reached out with its paw and laid it on top of both of their hands.

"You can understand me?" said the old lady, as she looked into Isabella's warm cobalt blue eyes "Nobody can under stand me."

"Yes mother I, that is we can understand you. So what do you think of your granddaughter?"

"She is so beautiful. How did you ever come up with such a heavenly name for her?"

"Mother, she's named after you."

The little old lady just sat there, with one hand holding the granddaughter named after her, and the other hand holding her daughters. While the little strange mouse was holding on to them all, its true arms wrapping them tight in a bear hug of love. Love from the husband, father and grandfather they all miss so much.

She had a name, Isabella and this little heavenly angel was named after her, the old lady just sat there looking back and forth from the little girl and her mother. Nether of the two la-dies and the little girl, say the little strange mouse as it slipped off the bench and made its way to the other side of the dirt path-way. It was time for him to go home, as it was time for them to go home as well. He stayed just long enough to see them off.

"Come mother, lets go home."

Isabella coughed again, uncontrollably for a few minutes, then stood up and started to take a step. Then she stopped to look back only once at the park bench. She leaned down and gave a soft kiss to her aged hand and then reached out to the small piece of wood, stroking it once more ever so gently. A little hand reached into her other hand and said "grandma, its time to go home."

Isabella looked into those cobalt blue is of her granddaughter and her large beautiful smile and said, "Yes, lets go home my dear sweet girl. You know I once new a little mouse and I called it Missy. I would very much like to call you Missy mouse if you don't mind."

"I would like that very much too, grandma." As she took her grandmothers hand.

Sofia pushed the rusted old cart to their car at the edge of the park, still running so it would be warm when they came back. Sofia had a smile on her face that wouldn't go away. She had found her mother in time and as she walked back to the car, she watched her mother and daughter humming in the setting suns light.

One old, walking as best as she could, and one young skipping while holding her newly found grandmothers hand. And she smiled even bigger, knowing this was right, this was good. Both of the Isabella's came to the overly large SUV, waiting to be taken home, too say goodbye to today, and to say good morning to a new day. A new life, one where they would never be apart and one where there would always be love and warm hugs and happy hearts.

"Come you two, get in its starting to get really cold out here," said Sofia, "oh, and if you girls play nice, I'll tell you a story of grandma and when she was a lady of business. A lady of power, who commanded hundreds of men in the old wall street, before the banks went under."

The SUV pulled away from the park with one in the front and two in the back lessoning to Sofia as she told stories of her mother and the amazing woman she was in your youth. The family drove away, a family that would forever be together no matter what may come in the near and distant future.

Nobody noticed two little feet sitting on his little rump, holding his other two paws as a single tear slid down his fading face. And as the sun came to an end of its day and the moon took over, only an outline of her lover was remained, as his soul scampered up the moons beam. On its way to Heaven, waiting for his lover to come home to him when it was her time to run up the moons beam, he would be waiting for her at the golden gates of Heaven everlasting embrace.

A bench sits alone in the setting sun, with a golden plate smeared a little, by the hands of a lover no longer in need of its warmth, faith and love.

So sit. Open that tinderbox of your lost faith, emotions and love, let this simple little bench refreshen your soul. And if anyone sits on this most amazing and strange little bench, they would see a golden plate on the backrest and in the middle they would see some strange squiggly words and a small saying at the bottom that reads. *"To my beloved, always yours."*

And to those who site on this worn out wooden bench, they would see and understand those squiggly words saying. *"Come have a seat and be filled by his love, for it flows through the wood of his calling. The wood of his life, and the wood that held his body and took his life."*

****

Today was a day just like any other for the rest of humanity, but to her it was to be a day of great importance, a day of miracles. One where a little mouse found his long lost love's daughter, and one where a daughter who so wanted to give back the love she took away so many years ago.

So I say to you. Do you walk by or do you interact with another person, any person no matter what you may see? Well do you?

The End?

52.

What do you know of true loneliness?
21 Feb 2017

The feeling of loneliness is like nothing I've ever felt before. Pain, hate, love, and all the other feeling one can feel, don't compare to the feeling of loneliness. And those who have never truly felt this, will never come to know, the raw and imperfect person, inside of themselves and us all.

Its only in these moments of complete singularity of ones self. That you become open to the void of creation... To the real you. You may not like what you find, you may come to hate the very existence of your birth and being. But if you can push through the blackness that tries to consume your very soul, you just may find the person you were meant to be.

That maybe, just maybe all the hardships and pain and especially the loneliness, was nothing more than a trial by fire. A cauldron of lost hopes, dreams and the illusion of what you thought was proper. In not only your thoughts but of other thoughts, of what was right, in what you were meant to be.

That this journey of darkness and misery, was the only road you could have ever walked in this life, for it was your destiny to be alone. To be the... alone. And by claiming your right to this void of your own creation, just maybe, salvation of your very soul is within arms reach. Maybe, just maybe become pure... perfect.

Becoming who you were meant to be. Own the darkness, claim the loneliness and make it bend to your will. Be not afraid to walk into the stygian blackness of your mind, for light and life await on the other side.

53.

What is true happines?
16 march 2020

Question:

Live life one second at a time, for when it's gone you'll never get it back. Immortality lies in a pure second of true happiness. But what is, living in the moment... living this very second, even mean?

It means:

To make a wish, hold it for a lifetime. Then throw it away, praying it will start over agian the very next day. And in that wish, you ponder a million chances... to do it all again. But, only right the next day.

A second, is a blessing. Given to all of the children of this Earth. In the hopes, that we will wish to do it all again. But in the right way and the right time. Without greed, anger and envy. Controlling the minds and hearts of humanity.

For you see. The light of humanity is that wish, becoming that second. If only we try.

54.

The pebble of change
02 Feb 2009

Part One

Sam Hatchens held the only known copy of The Prophecies of the Mad Monk. A man who lived up in the high peaks of the Japanese mountain. A volcano actually known as Mount Fuji. Where he wrote his abstract prophecies in the form of poetry. Telling of things to come. Mostly of destruction, death and change. Needless to say, his particular brand of prophecies were not well received. By any and all of the people of his time.

The only know scrolls in existence was found laying at the bottom of the ocean, in a sealed urn mixed in with a fortune of gold and jewels from an Italian pirate ship. Thought to be only a legend. A pirate ship that had come to the islands of Japan for pirating and slavery, on the pretense too trade in rare spices. It had reportedly sank in the year 1530 from a deadly hurricane that leveled the city of Tokyo, also known back then as Edo. Leveled not once but twice that century.

Legend had it that a mad monk from Italy had come to the islands of Japan on a slave trade boat. Taken from his family and forced to become a pirate upon pain of death to his family if he tried to escape. This monk, with no name. Came to the Japanese islands, he had spent two years aboard pirating and killing with the crew of the Italian trade and slave ship. Only to be thrown over board, after a bought of brain fever that had ran ramped, on his now home. The dreaded pirate ship known as "Sangue del mare", meaning Blood of the Sea in the English language.

****

The pebble of change
By: The Mad Monk
In the year of our Lord 1352

The turning of the universe, hangs on the precipice of a mad man controlling all we do and say. Waiting for two to come together upon a chance meeting with loneliness on the mind. Wanting nothing more than to be loved truly and completely, with every atom of their being.

So the pebble is flung into action, with hungry eyes viewing its path, to total destruction. Awaiting for two to come and set the wheel of change into production. Twelve, how I hate the twelve of the last month of the year. For never will there be a new day, a thirteenth or a new year. Once again the pebble comes, cleansing the third rock from the burning sun.

****

Sam read and re-read this small poem, the last of fifty known poems of this amazing profit. There was something strange and familiar at the same time with this poem, but for the life of Sam he couldn't figure out why. So he decided to email it to his friend Julie Walters, his mentor, friend and once lover. It had been more then ten years now since they were romantically involved with each other. It had been a college fling, but one that he had always looked upon with a wistful and misty eye.

Sam sent out the email to Julie asking for help, her to come to Japan to read the poems of the Mad Monk for herself. He knew his old mentor and that she was always doubting his research methods. She had told him the last day they saw each other, that he had become a fraud, a fake and a charlatan trying to con the archaeological world with his theories of this legend of the Mad Monk. Who prophesied the end of the world, in his abstract poetry.

Julie Walters was knee deep in the mud and muck of the South American rain forest, Guatemala to be exact, just south of Tikal temple. Where she has been looking for a tablet made from the bark of an ancient tree, that told of the location of a book made from the paper of a fig tree. A tree that the ancient Mayans used to make their sacred books from.

Books they bound with human flesh and inked in the blood of the people they sacrificed. Where they kept all their greatest incantations, rites, rituals and their most guarded secrets within. Then placed into a golden chest, covered with hieroglyphs of protection and power. Hieroglyphs that were placed by the high priestess during the first blood moon of the new year. Sacrificing multiple humans to the ancient Mayan Gods of their time.

The legend of the book became known to Julie more than twenty years ago, when she was working on her doctorate. Becoming obsessed with the book, consuming the focus of her life's work. Its rumored to be the first book to be created by the ancient Mayans, a book that foretells of the ending of the world.

Julies right pants pocket rang as she shifted her weight, trying to squeeze her way through the small fisher between the opening of a forgotten old Mayan temple, an into a extremely small little room. Julie pulled her Iphone out of her right leg pocket, an saw a text message from someone she never thought she would see or hear from again.

"Hay Jule's this is Sam. I found the scrolls of the Mad Monk, please come to Tokyo ASAP." Julie turned off her head lamp and phone saving the batteries and sat in the darkness of the extremely tight temple room she had just entered. In complete darkness, as the image of Sam came to her mind. Thinking to herself *"was this a trick, could it be true? No, it has to be a lie. But what if it isn't a lie, it could be a historically changing find. One that could spell the doom of all she has come to know and love."*

Julie turned her head lamp back on and looked around at the rubble standing in her way. Rubble that would have to be removed before she could go any further into the temple. Where she hoped to find her key to the golden chests location, holding an even greater treasure within.

With that said and done, she turned back around ready to once again face her fears. As she slid between the small crack, that lead her into the smaller fissure. That lead her to the opening and to the fresh air of the outside world. Where a very long trip to Tokyo awaited her and to the man she once loved, one Sam A. Hatchens.

Part Two

Fujimoto Turned around at the airport entrance taking a second look at the lady who passed across his view and held his breath as he thought to himself. *"Its Julie, but it couldn't be Julie. She said she would never come back to Japan and if she did she would never come to Tokyo. That it was over and she could never forgive him for his betrayal with his assistant who was only nineteen years old."*

Julie stopped at the same time as Fujimoto turned around, she had seen him too and couldn't believe her eyes. He was still the most beautiful man she had ever laid her eyes on and he was now walking her way. She instantly felt as if she was back in college and that feeling of being a small young girl from Texas. It was over powering.

She remembered that she found her teacher Mr. Suki Fujimoto, to be the most beautiful man she had ever seen, in her young nineteen years of life coming her way. Just as he was doing now, but back then she was a novice to the world and now it was very different. But Julie thought to herself as she watched his fluid movement and started to feel the melting of her legs as it did all those years ago. *"Its over Juls, its over. My god he looks good... its over! Or is it? No, No its defeinitely over, be strong Juls, be strong."*

"Hi, Juls."

"Hi, Suki."

They looked at each other for a few seconds. They could tell that the magic was still in the air. It hung there like the mistle-toe, when two people stand under it waiting for them to kiss each other. Fujimoto was about to say something, when Julie stopped him before he could even start. She told him she was here to see one of her colleagues, that he may have found a very rare document and that she would be back in town two days from now. If he wanted to see her they could meet at that res-taurant on Ying Lee street.

Fujimoto stood stunned for a second or two, then said only one word, yes. At hearing his yes, Julie smiled and turned around and walked away to go see Sam and this scroll from a mad monk almost seven hundred years ago.

She had rented an SUV from the airport and took off to find Sam, he had said he was at the foot of Mount Fuji. But he didn't say just where he was, he said he would call her when she was entering the area. He said he was not taking any chances, he also said it felt as if he was being followed. Julie found Sam at the foot of Mount Fuji after she called him when she was in the area, wrapping the scrolls in a water sealed container, then placing it into one of those new polyteflon mini safes.

Sam turned around at the sound of Julies voice and smiled, but she could see he was stressed out. Julie thought to herself,

"maybe he did find the actual scrolls. Or he was loosing his mind."
They spent the next two days looking over the scroll, at a
nearby local motel, trying in vain to decipher its code and its
authenticity.

They tried every type of code breaker they could think of, even
went as far as asking a few people they new in the hacking community for assistance. But nothing help, and the mysteries of
the Mad Monk would have to wait for now. Sam had a deadline
he needed to make, if he was going to get these scrolls out to the
academic community, before the end of the year. And then to
finally get the recognition he so deserved and wanted among
his fellow Archaeological community.

Sam said his goodbye's to Julie, wishing he could spent more
time with her and to maybe rejuvenate the old feelings. But
he call of making it big in the Archaeological community just
meant to much for him. Julie could see he was pulled from his
love to prove himself to the world and his continued feelings of
love for her. She made it easy for him, and said goodbye too and
turned around to and walked out of the motel room. Wanting
to see if there was anything left for her and Suki, or if it was to
late to rekindle old flames herself.

As Julie drove away she new at first glance that it was the real
thing, that he had actually done it he had found the Mad Monks
scrolls. She did the only things she could have done for him. She
gave him a written letter of Acknowledgment, saying that it
was the original works of the Mad Monk and that Sam Hatchens
was the finder and soul owner of the scrolls of the Mad Monk.

And as she drove off and looked at her watch, seeing it was the
Tenth of December, she wondered what the meaning of *"The
turning of the universe, hangs on the precipice of a mad man controlling all we do and say. Waiting for two to come together upon a
chance meeting with loneliness on the mind. Wanting nothing more*

than to be loved truly and completely, with every atom of their being. So the pebble is flung into action, with hungry eyes viewing its path, to total destruction. Awaiting for two to come and set the wheel of change into production. Twelve, how I hate the twelve of the last month of the year. For never will there be a new day, a thirteenth or a new year. Once again the pebble comes, cleansing the third rock from the burning sun." It was the only part of the scrolls that was written in English.

Fujimoto found her siting at their favorite restaurant, looking even more elegant then he remembered. They sat together ate lunch, but other things were on their minds. Seeing the same thoughts in the others eye, they left the restaurant and went to his place and had the most romantic, sensual and all consuming love the world would ever know. It was the Eleventh of December.

All the while this marathon of sex was going on. One was thinking of the Mad Monks sayings and what it could mean for the world. While the other was thinking that was it the right decision, in telling the president that it was the right thing for the human race. For him to press the button, sending the missile's on their journey into space. To destroy a rouge asteroid with an unknown element, one that could be the very thing the earth needs to save its failing fuel economy.

They were awoken to the sounds of thunder and lightning, it was the twelfth of December. And saw a single shining star falling from the heavens... And just then they both new.

Part Three

Sam looked at his calendar and thought to himself as he saw it was the eleventh of December. *"I need to get my paper sent out today, so I can get my credit which is long over due. In the finding of the Mad Monk's scrolls and the prophesied tellings of the end of the world. Yes its time the Archaeological world took me seriously and clear my name. Then Jules will now I've always loved her and it was that love for her that made me do the things I've done."*

Sam sent out his letter to the board of Archaeological Affairs, happy for the first time in the last ten years. Soon he would have his respect back and then he would make his way to Julie, to get his lover back. Sam took a look over to her picture, that sat on his fireplace mantle and smiled. Then turned off his computer and walked outside to sit on his Spanish tiled back porch, watching the stars and the full moon. As it rose into the cool, crisp winters night with the hint of snow on the breeze.

Sam couldn't remember what had happened, all he could remember was going to bed. Then a booming sound that deafening the ears and brought blood poring out of his eyes, nose and ears. He tried to sit up, but his rigs burned from trying in vain, to pull oxygen into his lungs. From the growing acid and sulfur that was coming from the crack at the bottom of his front door.

His single working eye focus's on two things at once. The twenty foot tall wall of living flame, walking its way to his once beautiful uptown New York-en home. The other to a simple piece of paper floating in front of him with the small saying, that gave the last human upon this doomed watery planet pause.

An in the aftermath of the small pebble sized asteroids impact. A small piece of New York Times newpaper floats before the growing flame that has become the new sunrise. And one small section of the newspaper becomes visible among the ever growing hunger of the eternal flame. That has come home, to reclaim its forgotten planet of water, dirt and air. The small piece of paper hovered in front of Sam's face and his one working eye. Floating, awaiting its turn to burn.

*** New York Times
Special Edition
12 December 2012***

"Come to New Your Time Square
and ring in the new year
with all your family and friends
saying goodbye...

The last part of the sentence was burned away, but the effect was not lost upon its reader. And the last thing the earth would ever hear, was the laughter of the last human as the Mad Monks poem came into his disintegrating mind. *"Twelve, how i hate the twelve of the last month of the old year, for never will there be a new day, a thirteenth or a new year."*

As the understanding came to his mind, he laughed once more as he drifted off into madness while the living wall of death washed over his warn and tired body and mind. For today was the twelfth of December, year two thousand and twelve.

****

For hell has come to claim the once beautiful third rock from the sun. In the form of a single pebble from a passing asteroid. That was rudely interrupted from its peaceful sailing across the void of time and space. minding its own business. The pebble sails into the planet called Earth, cleansing all its greedy and environmentally uncaring children. In its wake preparing the canvas for the hand of God. To try once again, with a new species of mankind.

Ding Dong. Welcome to the ringing of a new year!

The End

EPILOGUE

"So my lovelies, how did you like my work?"

"It was divine, sumptuously delicious my master."

"Did you find it helpful in your path back to the land of the living? Did you learn anything new, as your minds perused my learned craft?"

"Oh, yes my master. We have learned to once again raise our feet, tread out into the land of the living. To walk among those, who have found true peacefulness in ones own mind, body and soul."

"That is good, very good. And will you please stop calling me Master. No, wait... I think its growing on me."

"It is my master."

"Yes. Yes, keep calling me your Master. Keep calling me Master. My minions of the lost... my lovelies!"

ABOUT THE AUTHOR

L.f. Young

L.F. Young is a overly and abundantly giggly and silly person at times, who loves a great book to read. Cherishes the enjoyment of friends and loved ones... if he had any. And finds the time to play the occasional game or three, when not being engrossed in a new anime series or the rare TV show that isn't just a copy of ones from the past. A lover of KPop and any and all music from the dawning of time to the hear and now. With the few exceptions that I will keep to myself.

All in all, L.F. Young is a sweet, kind and loving person to any and all that I come across in this path called LIFE.